Welcome to the December 2008 collection of
Harlequin Presents!

This month, be sure to read Lynne Graham's
The Greek Tycoon's Disobedient Bride, the first
book in her exciting new trilogy, VIRGIN BRIDES,
ARROGANT HUSBANDS. Plus, don't miss the second
installment of Sandra Marton's THE SHEIKH TYCOONS
series, *The Sheikh's Rebellious Mistress.* Get whisked
off into a world of glamour, luxury and passion in
Abby Green's *The Mediterranean Billionaire's
Blackmail Bargain,* in which innocent Alicia finds
herself falling for hard-hearted Dante. Italian tycoon
Luca O'Hagan will stop at nothing to make Alice his
bride in Kim Lawrence's *The Italian's Secretary Bride,*
and in Helen Brooks's *Ruthless Tycoon, Innocent
Wife,* virgin Marianne Carr will do anything to save
her home, and ruthless Rafe Steed is on hand to help
her. Things begin to heat up at the office for interior
designer Merrow in Trish Wylie's *His Mistress,
His Terms,* when playboy Alex sets out to break
all the rules. Independent Cally will have one night
she'll never forget with bad-boy billionaire Blake in
Natalie Anderson's *Bought: One Night, One Marriage.*
And find out if Allie can thaw French doctor
Remy de Brizat's heart in Sara Craven's
Bride of Desire. Happy reading!

We'd love to hear what you think about Presents.
E-mail us at Presents@hmb.co.uk or join in the
discussions at www.iheartpresents.com and
www.sensationalromance.blogspot.com, where you'll
also find more information about books and authors!

Bedded by...

Blackmail

Forced to bed...then to wed?

He's got her firmly in his sights and she's got only one chance of survival—surrender to his blackmail...and him...in his bed!

Bedded by...**Blackmail**

The *big* miniseries from Harlequin Presents®

Dare you read it?

Abby Green

THE MEDITERRANEAN BILLIONAIRE'S BLACKMAIL BARGAIN

Bedded by...

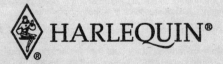

Blackmail
Forced to bed...then to wed?

HARLEQUIN®

TORONTO • NEW YORK • LONDON
AMSTERDAM • PARIS • SYDNEY • HAMBURG
STOCKHOLM • ATHENS • TOKYO • MILAN • MADRID
PRAGUE • WARSAW • BUDAPEST • AUCKLAND

ISBN-13: 978-0-373-12783-2
ISBN-10:   0-373-12783-9

THE MEDITERRANEAN BILLIONAIRE'S BLACKMAIL BARGAIN

First North American Publication 2008.

Copyright © 2008 by Abby Green.

All about the author...
Abby Green

ABBY GREEN deferred doing a social anthropology degree to work freelance as an assistant director in the Film and TV industry—which is a social study in itself! Since then it's been early starts, long hours and mucky fields, ugly car parks and wet-weather gear—especially working in Ireland. She has no bona fide qualifications but could probably help negotiate a peace agreement between two warring countries after years of dealing with recalcitrant actors.

She discovered a guide to writing romance one day, and decided to capitalize on her longtime love for Harlequin romances and attempt to follow in the footsteps of such authors as Kate Walker and Penny Jordan. She's enjoying the excuse to be paid to sit inside, away from the elements. She lives in Dublin and hopes that you will enjoy her stories.

You can e-mail her at abbygreen3@yahoo.co.uk.

CHAPTER ONE

'I AM quite certain that if I had fathered a child I would be well aware of the fact, which, needless to say, would be none of your business, as you are a complete stranger. Now take your hand off me immediately.'

Alicia Parker was still stunned into immobility by the sheer audacity of her actions, which had stopped this man in his tracks. She looked up into a face so savagely handsome that the breath left her body. All her poor muddled, overtired and over-wrought brain could formulate were impressions. Tall. Broad. Dark. Gorgeous. Sexy. Powerful. Sexy. Powerful.

Eyes as cold and dark as the night stared down with uncompromising arrogance and supreme assurance that she—and her preposterous accusation—were so far removed from his gilded life that she must be certifiably mad to accost him like this. His look could have turned her to ice…and yet, awfully, Alicia didn't feel cold. She felt hot. All over.

And as she watched, struck dumb by any number of things,

the very least of which was his overwhelming presence, Dante D'Aquanni calmly and disdainfully extricated the expensive cloth of his suit from her white knuckle grip, flicked a glance to his minions nearby and strode off and out of the mammoth building which housed his offices in London.

He was gone, as if spirited away, without a backward glance at the petite, dishevelled woman who stood gaping at his departing back. Who'd had only the briefest of chances to get out a few words, her attempt to make him listen having failed abysmally.

Within seconds Alicia was surrounded by great hulking security guards and, without knowing exactly how, she found herself outside in the teeming rain and what had just happened seemed like a blur…or a bad dream…

Alicia's soft mouth tightened into a grim line. Unfortunately, that day a week ago hadn't been a bad dream. It was a stark reality and the reason why she was now seated in a tiny rental car across the road from an exclusively opulent hotel near the shores of Lake Como in Italy. She even had the remnants of a cold as a result of getting soaked to the skin that day. Dante D'Aquanni had refused to hear her out then, but he wouldn't—couldn't—refuse to listen to her here…

The sun had set some hours ago, but the sky was still a dark, bruised violet colour. That magical moment when day teetered into night had come and gone, its beauty unnoticed. And, across the road, the hotel quite literally *glittered* with luxuriousness, adding to this heightened sense of beauty.

Alicia was terrified. She was trying not to be bowled over by it. Trying not to let the pristine streets intimidate her, the unmistakable handsome foreignness of the smartly dressed people coming in and out of the hotel. But still *not him…yet*. This was a million miles away from anywhere she'd ever been, or anywhere she was ever likely to be. She closed her eyes for a second; they were gritty with tiredness, every limb ached with exhaustion. She knew she wasn't far from collapse, but didn't have the luxury of time to sleep, to catch her breath. She was existing in a haze, anger at his recent curt dismissal and sheer nerves keeping her going.

This was the only solution, and the only way she was going to get to see him, *to force* him to admit his responsibility. To admit to fathering her sister's unborn child. A sudden image of Melanie's small, pale face against the hospital bed linen made Alicia's breath stop painfully. She closed her eyes but the image got stronger and she could see with alarming vividness, the scary profusion of tubes and wires that had snaked around her too thin body with its small bump. Alicia felt tears threaten; if *anything* happened to her... She couldn't let it. Her eyes snapped open. She needed money now for Melanie's treatment and Dante D'Aquanni *would* be made to accept the part he'd played in this chain of events. Would be made to pay. He was their only option. Alicia was desperate.

Her sister had been involved in a horrific car crash while on her way to see this very man and somehow, miraculously, she and her baby had survived. But she had suffered a fractured pelvis, among other more minor internal injuries. With the complication of being pregnant, the result was that they desperately needed to get Melanie into the care of a consultant who had expert experience with pregnancies which had suffered trauma. He was based in central London and Alicia knew well that this kind of care came privately and with a hefty price tag.

With no other close family and no friends who had anything approaching that kind of money to call upon, it had left her no choice but to take this course of action. The ward sister, an old friend of Alicia's from her nursing training days, had assured her that Melanie was stable and could be left for a short time. That assurance had led her to feel confident enough to make this drastic, desperate step, along with the promise that she would be notified the minute that any change occurred in Mel's condition.

She looked quickly at the hotel's intricately carved doors again, afraid that she might have missed him. Nothing. She'd followed him earlier from his villa on the shores of the lake to the hotel, where he had met a stunning brunette on the steps. She could only imagine what they would be doing now and wondered if Dante D'Aquanni would be taking her back to his villa or entertaining her in an opulent suite inside. Alicia worried her lower lip. She prayed that he wouldn't bring her back— Alicia needed him on his own.

Something caught the corner of her eye and she looked across the road again. A valet was bringing a low-slung, gleaming silver car to a halt outside the door, which was opening. Her eyes widened in apprehension—*his* car. And then he appeared. Mere feet away. Coming out of the hotel in a black tuxedo, the bow-tie undone at his neck. Certainly looking more dishevelled than when he'd gone in. The beautiful brunette accompanied him down the steps in a glittering silver sheath of a dress, also looking sexily tousled, long, dark lustrous hair around her shoulders. She looked thoroughly bedded.

Alicia wanted to feel revolted, but as she watched the woman twine sinuous arms around his neck and press close, all she did feel was a tingling awareness and something much more disturbing. She felt bewildered for a moment by the confusing emotion. The man's overpoweringly good looks and charisma, which she could remember like a brand from the previous week reached out to her from across the road.

Like any protective, loving older sister, she believed Melanie was beautiful and that everyone else loved her too…but Alicia knew well that she and her sister were not the type of women to turn this man's head. He was out of their league, on a level that hadn't even been invented yet. A grim hardness settled in her chest… *That was exactly why he had discarded Melanie with such callous ruthlessness.*

The valet had opened the driver's door of the open-top sports car. Dante D'Aquanni extricated himself from the woman and, with a brief kiss on her cheek, strode down the steps and to his car. After discreetly giving a tip to the valet, he slid into the driver's seat and, with a muted roar of the throttle, sped off.

The woman stood on the steps looking after the car, a look of comic chagrin on her beautiful face before she flounced back up the steps and disappeared, no doubt back to the suite from where they'd just emerged. It was only then that Alicia came to, shaken out of the crazy reverie that seemed to have taken hold. Hands shaking, she turned the key in the ignition and pulled out of her parking space. What was wrong with her? She needed all her concentration just to navigate in the unfamiliar car.

She breathed a sigh of relief when she saw red traffic lights ahead and the familiar lines of the powerful sports car. The light went green and he pulled off again.

She pictured all too easily the supreme nonchalance of his movements as he had come down the steps of the hotel just moments before. The way he'd coolly discarded the woman. It seemed to mock her now. This man didn't have a care in the world. So utterly confident that he could wreak havoc, walk away and believe himself to be protected.

Her phone rang shrilly on the seat beside her and she picked it up, listening for a second before saying briefly, 'Just follow me, I'll show you where we can get in.' She looked back and, sure enough, another car was not far behind. She cursed herself; she'd almost forgotten about the others. She couldn't let this man scramble her thoughts.

Fear gripped her at what she was about to do but she willed it down. She couldn't lose her bottle now. Not when she'd come so far. Not when she'd gone to so much trouble to find out where he was going on holiday, any one of his palatial homes being a possibility.

The road beside Lake Como at any other time might have been a magical route, but she couldn't enjoy the scenery, the way the rising moon was bathing everything in a dark, inky-blue light. All she could focus on were the car lights ahead of her.

She knew that the back of his villa faced on to the shores of the Lake, of which he had an unimpeded view. And that *apparently* one of his favourite times was dusk: he would watch the lights twinkle and come on across the still waters from his terrace, which was covered with antique drapes. Or at least that was the picture of the man that the gushing article had painted. Idyllic. A man who could have anything he desired at the click of his fingers. Alicia knew all about the exclusivity of the Lake Como villas. They were never advertised for sale, it was all word of mouth, buyers carefully vetted. And prices invariably soared into the high millions.

But then, for a multi-billionaire who controlled the largest, most successful construction company in the world, who would expect anything less? Her hands tightened on the steering wheel. She didn't imagine that he would have the callused hands of his workers.

His lights disappeared and Alicia had to concentrate. They were here, at the high wall of his villa. She cursed herself. She had to get it together. For Melanie. The effort it had taken her sister to say just a few words a week ago had been enough to tip her into unconsciousness. But they'd been enough.

They'd given Alicia all the information she'd needed.

She drove the car neatly into the space she had found earlier, partially hidden by an overhanging tree, and sat there for some moments waiting for the other car to draw up behind her. Alicia hadn't even known about Melanie's pregnancy until she'd come home from Africa and gone straight to the hospital after a series of panicky messages on her mobile and in their apartment had alerted her to her sister's whereabouts.

Since Melanie's best friend, the only other person likely to know her movements, was away on holiday, it had taken the hospital a day to properly identify Melanie and get in contact. And since that moment everything had been a scary blur. Alicia's thoughts revolved sickeningly on her sister's fevered words, which had led her to this place and this moment.

Melanie had gripped her hand, struggling to speak. It had made Alicia's heart break. 'Melanie, love, don't try to speak; you need to keep your strength.'

Melanie had shaken her head. 'I have to tell you. I have to see…have to talk to Dante D'Aquanni… He's the one…'

'Melanie—' Alicia's voice had been urgent '—what do you mean? Is he the one who did this to you? Is he the one you talked about?'

The communications between the remote area where she'd been working in Africa and the UK had been sporadic to say the least.

Melanie had sagged back against the pillows, her words were broken and her breath jagged. 'I was on my way to see him to tell him that I'd leave the company, do anything he wanted, if only to…I was so upset and then that lorry just came out of nowhere—' She closed her eyes at the memory, went paler and gripped Alicia's hand even tighter as her eyes opened again. 'You have to find him, Lissy…I need him to…' Alicia had been horrified to see weak tears rolling down her sister's face. 'Oh, Lissy, I love him so much and he sent him away…and I need him.'

Alicia's focus came back to the lake, lapping softly nearby. Her sister had been so feverish by then that she'd been incoherent, her words becoming jumbled. She'd obviously meant that he'd sent *her* away. The facts were stark and Alicia had pieced them together with little effort.

Her sister had had an affair with Dante D'Aquanni, the owner of the corporation she worked for. He had cast her aside. Melanie had been on her way to see him when the accident happened. She'd been made careless by her distraught state. Alicia's insides roiled again; she felt so guilty that she hadn't been there. She could have prevented the accident. If only she'd been able to phone more frequently. All she knew was that Melanie had been seeing someone at work. Her e-mails had been like Morse code, in an obvious effort to protect the man who had stolen her heart…her innocence.

After trying and failing to get in touch with Melanie's friend, who might possibly know more, Alicia had turned to the Internet to find out what she could about this man. She'd seen that office affairs within the D'Aquanni corporation were sackable offences—hence Melanie's ridiculously secretive e-mails—and yet the man himself had seen fit to be a hypocrite of the highest order...

A car door slammed behind her. She pulled back her mass of unruly hair and twisted it up, tying it with a band, putting on a battered baseball hat. Then she got out of the car, easing cramped muscles. The late summer air held the slightest of chills and she pulled on her voluminous dark sweatshirt. Then, taking her small backpack, making sure she had her phone and that it was on silent, she made her way to the two men who had just emerged from the other car.

Dante D'Aquanni drove his car to an abrupt stop on the gravel outside his villa. The feeling of relief was enormous. He vaulted out and ran up the few stone steps, his housekeeper coming out to meet him. They exchanged a few words and he strode through the open door and into the immense, palatial villa. Home. His favourite place in the world.

He recalled Alessandra's pleas to bring her back with him for the night. How she'd whispered what she'd thought were erotic promises into his ear on the steps of the hotel, but which had made any possible lingering desire disappear completely.

He poured himself a drink and took it to the back terrace where the view of the still, dark lake acted like a balm. Alessandra Macchi was indisputably one of the most beautiful women in Italy. And she had made no secret of the fact that she desired Dante. His mouth tightened. Desired his wealth. That much was clear. When he'd arrived at Lake Como a few days ago, he'd gone for a quiet drink, a catch up with some locals, and Alessandra had appeared with some flimsy story of taking a break too... She'd proved a force to be reckoned with. His defences must have been down, or something, as he'd found himself going to her hotel this evening to take her for dinner and then had allowed her to seduce him. He rubbed a weary hand across his brow.

What was wrong with him? He didn't normally regret anything he did, as each and every decision was made with full weighing up of pros and cons. Alessandra was exactly the type of woman he normally went for. Beautiful. Polished. Experienced. Not into commitment or, at least, he thought cynically, she *professed* not to be. So why had this whole evening been so wholly unspectacular? So…mechanical, unsatisfactory…

And when she'd wanted to come back *here*… He had to repress a shudder again at the thought. She hadn't been happy to be left on the steps of the hotel but he could be ruthless when necessary and knew women like her… She'd survive.

Congratulating himself on his escape, he downed the rest of the liquid and strode back through the villa. He could hear raised voices and see his housekeeper at the door. She looked as if she was struggling with something—*someone*—trying to get in.

Every instinct jumped to high alert. His whole body tensed—something that hadn't happened in a long time. It immediately brought back the memory of the constant dangers of living on the streets in Naples. Which was crazy. That was another world, a distant memory, *another life*. He was protected from that life now.

Alicia was trying to calm things down but the reporter and photographer that she'd brought with her were being aggressive. She was out of her depth, she was no con artist. The poor housekeeper was looking terrified as she tried to shut the door in their faces. Alicia had no Italian vocabulary to reassure her, to explain that all they wanted was to see Dante D'Aquanni. And she knew it would only be a matter of time before the guard at the gate found them.

Even though they had been able to get through the hole in the wall that she had found earlier and clamber through prickly bushes and trees, Alicia didn't doubt for a second that security here was state of the art. The photographer made a lunge for the door again and knocked Alicia's head, her hat sailed off and at that moment the door swung back and everyone stopped moving.

Dante D'Aquanni stood there, resplendent and devastating. Dark, dark eyes expertly assessing and taking in the small, bed-raggled group. He issued a few curt words and the housekeeper disappeared behind him. He came out and shut the door.

Words were locked in Alicia's throat. Like last week, she felt overwhelmed, ineffectual. Impotent. Would he recognize her?

He looked calm, yet Alicia could feel the barely leashed energy emanating from him in hypnotic waves. He folded his arms with an insouciance that said he'd summed them all up and found no threat. His gaze came to rest on her. And her heart stopped. She gulped.

The reporter's voice came from behind her. 'Signore D'Aquanni, do you know this woman?'

The first initial beat of danger that had surged through Dante was gone. He knew the local paparazzi. They were rabble. What he did feel now was anger that they were contaminating his property, and the reason they were here had to be this woman. His gaze slid up and down and a prickling sensation caught the back of his neck. An image crashed into his head.

Last week. At his offices in London. *This* woman had been there. She had emerged from behind a column, right in his path. He'd almost knocked her over, she was so tiny. The impression he'd formulated last week was the same as now and surprised him with its strength; he hadn't realized that he'd even taken that much notice. His eyes ran up and down her form. Not an ounce of femininity. Her scraped back hair was like the rest of her—of indeterminate colour, texture and shape.

Yet, to his surprise, even as he formulated that thought, he noticed big, wide-spaced brown eyes, ringed with long lashes that looked at him like a startled fawn. No threat.

'Yes,' he drawled with a measure of surprise, 'I believe I do.'
So he did recognize her.

Did he remember what she'd said? Alicia shook herself free of the overpowering intimidation that threatened to keep her silent. This was her moment, her chance. Even if he threw them all out and they didn't get pictures, the reporter would have a story and Dante would be forced into the limelight to at least acknowledge it on some level. He would be forced to think of Melanie then. She thought of her sister. She thought of the way he'd dismissed her last week and his *lover* so recently. She opened her mouth but before she could say a word, the reporter jostled forward roughly. 'Your little friend here tells us that she has a juicy story about you.'

Dante stiffened inside. He could see the woman's mouth open to speak, the spark of rage in her eyes and in a flash he also remembered the words she'd hurled at him last week. His head had been full of the upcoming negotiations, which was how she'd caught him slightly off guard.

'You're the father of my sister's baby and if you think you can walk away without accepting responsibility then you've another think coming.'

It had been such a preposterous accusation that he'd barely acknowledged her or her words. He didn't even have to think about it; he hadn't been seeing anyone in England and knew exactly who his recent lovers had been and not one of them would be remotely related to *her.* He was a billionaire; his lovers were carefully chosen and he was always, without fail, supremely careful to avoid such a scenario. Many women had attempted to trap him, lure him, and this woman was no different. He didn't have the time to try and figure out where she'd come from, if she was an employee…

Assimilating all this information in a split second, he also realized quickly that she evidently meant business as she'd followed him all the way to Lake Como. And, more importantly, he instantly assessed the damage she could do with her foolish audacity.

He had to stop her.

Alicia seized the opportunity she'd come so far for with both hands. 'This man,' she started bravely, but her voice sounded husky with the remnants of her cold. A dog suddenly barked halting her words. Her head whipped around. A security man held the dog back with a straining leash. She couldn't let this stop her. She faced back to Dante D'Aquanni. Desperation fuelling her movements, she squared her small defiant chin.

'*This man...*' It came out stronger this time and the dog mercifully stopped barking. The two men who'd followed her here looked at her eagerly, sensing a huge story in the offing. In that instant she regretted not having told them her story before now, she'd judged that the shock value would be greater, have more impact this way. She only hoped and prayed she could get it out.

'This man is responsible for—'

Before her lips could utter another word, they were smothered and stopped under a cruel, hard mouth. The world went dark and disorientation took over. Shock rendered Alicia stiff under the onslaught. It was comprehensive. Dante D'Aquanni crowded her, wrapped those strong arms around her, pulling her off her feet and into his chest. Her senses were so overloaded that she had trouble disentangling the strands of sensation.

There was his smell...musky and hot. There was the feel of his chest...hard, taut, unyielding. There was his firm mouth... touching, exploring. Suddenly she didn't feel stiff any more; she was melting, unable to stop the flood of heat to every part of her. His tongue was a silky, heated invasion that he pushed past shocked opening lips that belonged to someone else, not to her. Because, right now, she didn't inhabit her own body any more; it was someone else. Someone who had gone temporarily mad.

Dante lifted his head and it felt heavy. The clear, concise reasons for doing what he'd just done were unavailable to him now as he looked down into a grimy face, streaked with blood where she'd been struck by branches from the trees surrounding his property. Huge, liquid brown eyes stared up at him, lashes tangled and even more luxuriant up close. Lush lips were plump and pink. Quivering. Her whole body trembled in his arms; her hands were curled into his chest. *Where* had this nymph come from? Had the whole world gone mad in just an hour?

The security guard shouted something and Dante felt the return of sanity. He realized that he was holding this woman off the ground, into his chest and, as he lowered her back down with an abruptness that bordered on dropping her, he had to acknowledge the fact that he was aroused to a point that had most definitely eluded him earlier.

He knew that as much as he wanted to fling this stranger down his steps to join the paparazzi, something more compelling was stopping him. He also couldn't figure out his instinctive reaction to shut her up in any way possible, or why kissing her had been the only option.

The security guard surged forward and caught the two men by the scruffs of their necks, holding them easily. The reporter shouted out, 'Mr D'Aquanni, you were spotted with Alessandra Macchi earlier. What does this mean? Aren't you going to tell me who your new girlfriend is? It won't take long to find out…'

A curt, No Comment hovered on his lips but for some reason Dante didn't say it. He was certain of one thing. He couldn't let this woman go now because she was a loose cannon. Her determination to confront him told him he would be foolish to dismiss her so quickly this time. He had to get to the bottom of the preposterous allegations she had made—*was* making—and he welcomed the clarity that reminded him that at all costs he had to avoid any unwelcome press attention in the run up to the vital business negotiations next week. What the hell was wrong with him? Acting so out of character made him very nervous. He focused his mind again with effort.

He knew that his security guard would confiscate the camera, delete the digital images which had surely been taken, but, with technology being what it was, he knew he couldn't be certain they wouldn't have obtained an image of that kiss another way.

He had just kissed her in front of these men, they didn't need an image… This all flashed through his head in a nanosecond.

'Wait.' Dante's voice cracked out. The security man halted.

Alicia was taking all this in but she felt disembodied. His kiss—if you could even call it that—had seared its way into her blood, into her brain, and had lobotomized her ability to speak or function. All she could do was watch helplessly as Dante pulled her tight into his side.

He smiled urbanely, dangerously. 'I'm afraid that it's really quite banal. You've been used as a pawn in a lovers' spat. It's true I was out with Alessandra earlier. She, I'm afraid, was my attempt to make this woman jealous.' He looked down at Alicia and lifted her hand. It was held in a death grip; she could feel the blood stopping. But to their small audience it must have looked like a tender gesture when he brushed his mouth across her scratched knuckles.

'And it worked.'

The reporter's mouth was a round O of shock—presumably, Alicia thought for one clear second, that someone like her had the power to turn his head at all. She would have reacted the same way.

Dante D'Aquanni could have been Oscar nominated, the way he looked away from Alicia with extreme reluctance, but with what *she* could see very clearly was extreme loathing. His eyes were dark and hard.

The reporter shouted out, 'Where has she come from?'

'Come now, a man has to keep some things secret. Do you not think after all these years that I'd have a few evasive tricks up my sleeve? And do you really think that we could have made anything of this relationship if you'd known that I was seeing someone new, someone *serious?*'

Alicia was so stunned that she couldn't even begin to see how she could possibly get out of this mess.

Dante *hated* the woman at his side with a vengeance for bringing this intrusion into his life. How dare she? He was caught between a rock and a hard place. The reporter had his story anyway and if Dante called the police in it would fan the flames of a news item that didn't even exist!

He smiled again and it was cold. 'Needless to say, this will be the last time you invade my privacy and if I catch you even attempting to trespass again, you will pay the price.' Dante tightened his hold on Alicia, making her gasp painfully. 'You're lucky that love is making me magnanimous.'

And with that the reporter and his companion were summarily marched down the driveway. Alicia's legs were very wobbly and she had a taste of just how stupid she'd been in thinking for a second that it had been easy to get in. She'd just been very, very lucky.

CHAPTER TWO

ALICIA FELT ANYTHING but lucky now, though, as her head swirled with everything that had just happened and Dante D'Aquanni dropped his hands as though she were infectious.

'Get inside. Now.'

Alicia opened her mouth. He made a move and she flinched. She didn't know this man, didn't know his capacity or otherwise for violence and, right now, he looked murderous.

'Not a word, lady. Inside. Now.'

Alicia walked into the villa on cotton wool legs. She saw a chair and went and sat down, seriously afraid that she might fall.

'Get up. Did I say you could sit down?'

Alicia looked up, her face leached of all colour. 'Please… I—'

Dante strode forward and pulled her out of the chair. Two hands on her arms, holding her like a rag doll. And she felt like a rag doll.

'How dare you? How *dare* you invade my private space,

bring those miscreants onto my property, a *photographer* for heaven's sake—'

Alicia looked up into the harsh features—no less handsome now because of his anger. Even more mesmerizing because of it. From some reserve she called up her own anger, which had been in woefully short supply for the past few minutes. He might have turned the tables but she was still here. He hadn't turfed her out on the road.

'I dare, Mr D'Aquanni, because someone I love very much is lying in a hospital bed and she needs help. Help that I can't give her. As much as it kills me to come here and have to deal with someone as amoral as you, I have no choice.' Bitterness laced her words. 'Believe me, it's not my idea of fun scrabbling around thorn bushes in the dark. I *did* try to talk to you last week, if you recall, but you wouldn't listen.'

He delivered a scathing glance up and down. 'I don't have time to waste, listening to someone shrieking such unfounded accusations.'

Alicia remembered the panic that had galvanized her actions, the fear that had been barely in check when she'd seen him. She'd had to stop him somehow and, as much as she might have wanted to be civil, she hadn't been allowed. She strove for calm now.

'I *tried* to make an appointment to see you in your office but it would have been easier to get an audience with the Pope.'

He snorted inelegantly and in the next second moved so fast that Alicia was caught totally by surprise.

He had slipped her bag from her shoulders and upended it on to the floor in seconds. After a moment of shock she stepped forward. 'How dare you—'

But he held her back easily with one hand and the feel of that hand against her belly made her jump back like a scalded cat.

She watched as he flicked through the contents of her bag. Her wallet had a shockingly small amount of money. The printout of her one way ticket to Milan—she hadn't been able to get a return as the world and its wife were there that weekend for a football game. Her phone. A credit card.

Dante threw the paltry things back into her holdall and stood easily, towering over her as he inspected her driver's licence. He quirked a brow and looked at her.

'Alicia Parker…'

She nodded jerkily. Surely the name would register with him? It didn't seem to. He advanced dangerously and she moved back, feeling more and more light-headed.

'So, what exactly are you up to, coming here with a one-way ticket? Were you hoping your little trip would be so successful that you'd score a lift back on my private jet…or score *me?* Is that your plan? To seduce me and really get pregnant so your bizarre claims are founded on truth?'

Alicia's mouth opened but, before she could say a word, he was continuing, his words falling and stinging her flesh.

'If that was what you'd planned, then you're doing a woeful job. I don't go for dramatics and unkempt shrieking fishwives are not my type.'

Alicia stopped moving. She glared up at him, adrenalin surging through her quivering five foot two frame. Her voice shook with emotion.

'Melanie. Melanie Parker is her name. Does that even ring a bell with you? Or do you categorize your lovers by their social standing, in which case I'd imagine Melanie came somewhere near the bottom of the heap—'

'What did you say?' he asked sharply, stopping in his tracks.

Alicia was stymied for a second. He looked genuinely confused. And then she did see a flicker of something cross his face. Recognition. Anger surged all over again; apparently Melanie hadn't made that much of an impression.

'You are unbelievable. You can sleep with someone and not even recall their name unless pushed?'

He closed the distance between them and took her shoulders roughly. She bit back a gasp. As if he realized how delicate she was, he dropped his hands abruptly and she stumbled back, but kept standing even though everything swayed ominously for a second. She could not be weak. Not here, not now. She had to be strong for Melanie.

Dante's face felt rigid with rage and anger. He didn't believe what she said for a second…but that name…it did ring a bell— a loud one. Not that he was going to admit that now, not until he had more independently trustworthy information. This woman was up to something and he felt very sure it had to do with money.

He enunciated his words very slowly. 'Be clear. I have very little patience left. What is it you want?'

Alicia tilted her chin up and she unconsciously confirmed his prediction. 'What I want, Mr D'Aquanni, is money. I need money for my sister's care. If you don't give it to me—to us—then her unborn child is in serious danger of not coming to term.' Her voice shook ominously. '*Your baby.* Or don't you even care about that?'

Dante frowned. 'What on earth are you talking about, woman?' She was talking in riddles. Perhaps she was a little crazy? She also looked as if a gust of wind would knock her down and he steeled himself not to give in to the delicate image she was trying to project.

'*Care*—what are you talking about?'

The harsh quality of his voice shocked Alicia out of the stupor that had rendered her momentarily speechless. Of course. How would he know that Melanie had been in the accident?

She spoke, but increasingly she was feeling more and more detached from her body. 'Melanie…Melanie was in an accident. She was on her way to see you, and a lorry skidded on the motorway in front of her; it jackknifed right back—'

At that moment everything seemed to hit Alicia at once. The magnitude of what she'd just done. What she'd been through in the past week since she'd arrived home from Africa. The fact that she was here. What had just happened out on the front steps.

Had he really kissed her? And had she clung to him so help-lessly?

The hall around her swayed, went into double vision, and this time she couldn't stop it.

When she came round, she was sitting on the chair with her head between her legs, a large hand clamped to the back of her neck. She was mortified and felt like protesting vociferously—she didn't faint! She'd been through unspeakable horrors in the last year and had developed nerves of steel. And yet here, surrounded by luxury, she'd fainted within minutes.

Alicia saw the black clothed legs and shoes of Dante D'Aquanni beside her. She saw another pair of feet. She muttered something unintelligible and tried to move. The pressure of the hand eased. *His* hand. She looked up; the kindly, matronly face of the housekeeper looked at her. She felt like crying. They spoke in Italian above her head.

With little ceremony she was pulled up again, her head swam and, before she knew which way was up, she was over Dante D'Aquanni's shoulder, dangling inelegantly against his back. He strode across the hall and started climbing stairs.

'What the hell do you think you're—?'

'Be quiet. This will help the blood get to your head and restrain me from doing something I've never been tempted into before. When was the last time you ate or were you so consumed with gold-digging that you forgot?'

Alicia's hands were balled into fists as she couldn't look anywhere but at the man's perfectly shaped behind, his back against which her breasts were crushed.

'Gold-digging? *Gold-digging?* How dare you? Have you even considered the havoc that you've caused in my sister's—'

And, just as suddenly as she had been picked up, she was back on her feet, the rush of blood to her brain making her dizzy all over again. She put a hand to her head. She was barely aware of standing in a huge bedroom, discreetly designed with understated elegance and extreme luxury.

Dante was walking away from her. She ran after him. 'Wait

a minute. I'm not finished. What are you going to do about my sister? You can't ignore me.'

He turned, with his hand on the doorknob. His mouth was tight. 'No, you've made that impossible. But what I can do for now, and what I am going to do, is lock you in here.'

Alicia's mouth opened and closed. 'You…what…you're not going to…'

'Oh, yes, I am.'

And then he walked out, the door shutting ominously behind him. Stupefied, Alicia heard a key turn. She ran to the door, jiggled the knob. He had done it. He had locked her in.

She beat on the huge, heavy door with tiny fists. 'Come back here! You can't just lock me away. This is outrageous.'

Nothing. Not a sound. He was gone. Alicia sank back against the door and slid to the ground in a heap. She didn't have a thing. Not even her phone to try and get help. And who would she call? Her only relative lay unconscious in a hospital bed in England. She didn't need a friend to tell her what she already knew. She'd trespassed on the property of one of the most powerful men in the world. He had every right to go and call the police, which was probably exactly where he had gone. Any accusation she could level at him regarding her sister would be her word against his right now. Her brave, stupid mission had just gone up in flames. She should never have left England, never left her sister's side.

The article she'd read on the Internet mocked her. In her frantic research after he'd refused to see her, listen to her, she'd come across a particularly bitter piece by a jilted lover, or *alleged lover* as the article had been careful to state, ever mindful of litigation, especially where a billionaire was concerned. However, the woman was one of many, it seemed. It was what she had said that had galvanized Alicia to take these drastic actions. The woman had said that the only way to deal with a man like Dante D'Aquanni was by taking him by surprise, hitting him where it hurt. Publicly. Even super successful businessmen weren't immune to public opinion. Public censure. And if people knew that he'd callously turned his back on a pregnant ex-lover—

A brief knock came on the door at that moment and Alicia scrambled up. Maybe she'd been too harsh, maybe he'd listen if she tried to be reasonable. The key turned and the door opened. Alicia's hands were clasped in front of her. 'Look, I'm sorry for—'

But it wasn't Dante D'Aquanni. It was the kindly housekeeper. She came in with a tray that held a steaming bowl of pasta and a glass of water. Alicia was so shocked that all she could do was stare, it didn't even occur to her to try and escape. Her hollow stomach rumbled.

The woman smiled, her eyes crinkling in her brown face, seemingly oblivious that Alicia was no *guest* of the master. She put down the tray and gestured to Alicia's clothes. She obviously meant for her to take them off. Alicia backed away and put her hands up.

'No, no…they're fine, really…' She wished she knew some Italian. But the woman was clearly not taking no for an answer. She took Alicia by the hand and led her to the bed, pulling her sweatshirt up and, before Alicia could protest, too weak in all honesty, the woman had whipped it off.

Her trousers were next and soon she stood in just her underwear. The woman pointed at the tray, which also held some cotton wool and antiseptic. She gestured to the cut on Alicia's face and tutted. Alicia touched it, feeling the raised and congealed welt. She hadn't even noticed. The housekeeper disappeared into an *en suite* bathroom and returned with a luxurious white robe, which she left on the bed.

Then she gathered up Alicia's clothes and left the room, the ominous turning of the key making her come to her senses again. Nothing had changed; she was still a prisoner. She sat on the bed, arms wrapped around herself. She wanted to ignore the plate piled high with fragrant, steaming pasta. Wanted to conduct a hunger strike. But she knew how weakened she was. She needed her strength to be able to deal with Dante D'Aquanni again.

And when she saw her reflection in the mirror of the bathroom a short time later, she was glad she had eaten because she nearly fainted all over again at the sight of the scarecrow that greeted her.

Dante turned the key quietly and opened the door. It was much later that night. The light in the room was dim. He walked in and stood by the bed, hands deep in the pockets of his trousers. He had convinced himself that what had happened to him when he'd kissed the woman earlier had been as a result of the surreal circumstances. But now, as he looked down at her, he felt a disconcerting pulse throb to life in his blood. For a screaming virago, there was something curiously innocent about her.

In a bathrobe which swamped her petite frame, her hair was no longer an indistinct bundled up mess. It was a mass of dark blonde ringlets spread on the pillow behind her. With the grime and dust washed away he could see her face properly for the first time; she was actually extremely pretty.

She looked as if she'd gone to sleep despite herself, as if she'd fought it. Her hands were balled up, making her look as if she was ready, even now, to take on some attacker. The raised red welt on her cheek made him feel curiously concerned. He cursed himself.

His gaze travelled down; one slim leg, with a perfectly shaped calf and silky-smooth skin peeped out from the folds of the robe. Her foot was *tiny,* no bigger than a child's. Her breaths were deep and even. She was in a heavy sleep and had been for hours. He knew, as his housekeeper had informed him. This perplexed him. It didn't fit with the image of someone who'd just trespassed and hurled accusations at him concerning paternity. If anything, it damned her more because she was obviously complacent enough to sleep.

He tensed almost violently when she muttered something in her sleep and moved restlessly. When she settled again, the robe had gaped open and one small, yet surprisingly lush breast was bared. Crowned with a dusky pink crest, the slope was pert and curved so enticingly that Dante stared, transfixed and shocked, as *that* desire rocked through his body again and he had a sudden urgent hunger to rouse that tip to hard life, to see the rest of her naked body. It was a totally inappropriate and unwelcome desire.

Again the insidious thought mocked him—*this* was the kind of desire that had proved so elusive that evening. The kind of desire he hadn't felt for so long that he almost didn't recognize it. It was primitive, guttural, base. Far from his initial conviction that she wasn't feminine, the sleeping form of the woman screamed with a delicately curved femininity that he'd never encountered. And he could remember all too well how easy it had been to lift her slight form against his body, how she'd felt, how those soft, warm lips had opened up beneath his own…

That thought, and his fast growing arousal, propelled Dante back from the bed and out of the room, closing the door, his hand turning the key in the lock quickly, almost as if the woman on the other side was a witch who would materialize in front of him.

When he got to the bottom of the staircase his security guard was waiting, still looking shamefaced after having had to search and find the breach in security. He handed Dante a folder. 'The information you were looking for. She's related to a Melanie Parker who works in your London offices. Alicia Parker is a qualified nurse, and in the last twelve months there were at least six nurses called A Parker registered in various places, from a private nursing home in Devon to a relief organization in Africa. Within twenty four hours we should know which one she is.'

Dante took the folder and flipped it open, not one shred of the surprise he felt at learning this information showing on his impassive face. He'd know a lot more than that in twenty four hours. 'That'll be all for now.'

He went into his study and poured himself a measure of

cognac. Sitting down at his desk, he flicked through the papers. After a while he sat back and looked out of the huge window which had a view over the darkened lake, the glass in his hand. He was glad he'd followed his instincts in not calling the police straight away.

Much to his chagrin, he had to concede that she hadn't been talking complete gibberish. He ran a hand around the back of his neck. Unfortunately, he knew exactly who Melanie Parker was. And, if what this woman said was true—if her sister was in hospital, claiming to be *pregnant*—then things could get very sticky. Obviously the Parker sisters were going for the jugular. Who else knew about this? There was only one thing to do. He would have to keep Alicia Parker close, until he got to the bottom of this mess and discovered the real truth. Until he found out exactly what it would take to nip this in the bud.

His mouth twisted after he downed the last of the dark liquid. With the news of his new *love affair* no doubt hitting the newsstands within the next twelve hours, it wouldn't be hard to keep her close. A sudden image of her naked breast made his hand tighten on the glass. The last thing he needed right now was a libido brought to life by this…*stranger* who was threatening the equilibrium he so favoured in his life. But already his blood felt hot running through his veins, his heart picked up a rhythm and, as if possessed, when he closed his eyes all he could imagine was going back upstairs, wrapping a long skein of rippling hair around his hand, bending down and taking that lush, soft mouth with his. He wanted to taste her again, wondered if she would feel tight around him…

Not used to such carnal images invading his thoughts, he stood, agitated, and strode across the room, poured himself another shot, swallowing it back in one gulp. There was no doubt about it, they must be working as a team, the two sisters, or friends, whatever they were. It wasn't even a particularly sophisticated scam, but it was a scam nonetheless and one he would reveal quite effortlessly. His insides lurched at the thought that someone believed he could be stung—*again*.

He'd learnt his lesson the first time round.

This was not the time to become embroiled in some tabloid hell, fielding false accusations of fatherhood. These women— Alicia Parker and Melanie Parker—were obviously determined to see him publicly humiliated in order to extract money and, with the negotiations so close, no doubt the story of the accident was a ruse to inspire urgency.

If there was ever a time in his life when he needed calm waters, this was it. Too many people depended on him to let a stupid news story created by gold-diggers mess things up. He walked back to the desk and picked up the phone, making the first of a few calls.

CHAPTER THREE

ALICIA stood by the window, the spectacular view outside going unnoticed. It was early the following morning. She was back in her own freshly laundered clothes. She'd tied her hair back in a plait and it hung down her back, between her shoulder blades. She felt tense and worried, wanted to call the hospital to see how Melanie was, see if she'd woken up.

In the cold light of day she couldn't believe everything that had happened. And couldn't believe that she'd slept for almost eight hours straight. Dead to the world. In *his* house. She'd fought the tiredness for the longest time, sitting on the floor with her back against the wall, watching the door, but her eyes had kept closing, her head jerking.

She'd tried not to give in, had told herself that she'd only close her eyes for a few minutes…but, unable to resist the lure of hot water, even just washing her face and rinsing out her underwear, the soft robe, the even softer bed…she'd fallen into the abyss that had been calling her for weeks now. Here of all places—some protective older sister that made her. Maybe it was the effects of her lingering cold as well. She was useless. She should never have come, never have left—

The key turned in the lock and she jumped around, her heart lurching crazily. Dante D'Aquanni stood in the doorway. He took her breath away. He was even more shockingly handsome in the stark daylight. Dressed in black trousers, a dark grey shirt, he looked effortlessly cool, stylish and very much the successful businessman. And he also looked extremely annoyed. Any wish to try and make him see reason flew out of the window and Alicia felt her spine straighten; the familiar pain in her lower back made itself felt again, like a dull ache. She knew she shouldn't have been doing so much, not to mention scrambling through bushes, only to be thrown over this man's shoulder. Her insides went hot at the thought of that, cancelling out the pain.

'Mr D'Aquanni—'

He lifted a terse hand, halting her in her tracks when she took a tentative step forward. He came into the room with her bag and held out her phone. She reached for them eagerly. Her phone was still on silent and on the screen there were numerous missed calls listed, all from the hospital. Her bag fell out of nerveless fingers. Her face went white as she forgot everything and dialled the number.

Turning her back on Dante, she asked for the ward sister when a voice answered. What she heard when the woman came on the line made her eyes close and she said a few shaken words.

After cutting the connection she turned to face Dante D'Aquanni and he was surprised to see moisture in her eyes. He hadn't been expecting that. He still felt slightly winded at seeing her just now, in the clear light of day. That mass of curly hair was pulled back, yet some tendrils of silky spirals were coming loose. Her eyes were huge—almost too big for her small, heart-shaped face—and dark brown. Like velvet. It was hard to focus for a second.

But, as if he'd imagined it, the sheen of moisture in her eyes was gone, blinked away. She reminded him of a hissing kitten and he felt, above anything else, a curious need to reassure, protect. He had to smile inwardly to himself. She was certainly putting on a show worthy of an award—some operator.

Panic mixed with relief made Alicia's voice feel constricted. The connection had been bad but she'd heard enough. 'That was the hospital; they've been trying to reach me. My sister has woken up and she's asking for me, I have to go to her now.' *She'd worry about how later...* This whole plan had been an unmitigated disaster and Alicia could only hope that Dante would let her go.

'I know,' he said curtly. The deep timbre of his voice resonated within her like some kind of sensual pull on her senses. It took a second for his words to sink in. *He knew*?

Dante's mouth tightened to a harsh line. Now that he'd had a glimpse of what was underneath the baggy clothes, he couldn't be unaware of the effects, which gripped him with surprising and unwelcome force.

Alicia looked up into dark eyes. When had he moved so close that she could touch him? She frowned slightly, annoyed that he could be so cool, calm, unflappable.

'*How* do you know?'

A muscle flickered in his jaw. 'There's plenty I know, Miss Parker. And there's plenty more I'm going to know when we get to England.'

Relief flooded her, even as something very contradictory and ugly raised its head in the pit of her belly. 'You mean, you agree? That is, you're not going to deny that you're the father any more?'

He shook his head abruptly, irritation flashing across his face. He could practically see the pound signs in her devious eyes. 'No. That's where you're still wrong. There is no doubt in my mind that I am not the father of your sister's baby. That is if she is even pregnant.'

Alicia bristled, incensed that he could still be denying it. 'Of course she's pregnant; she has a bump for crying out loud. She is not a liar. You *are* the father. She specifically told me—'

He swiped his hand again. 'If she did then she's lying. This conversation is boring me. Let's go.'

He turned and walked from the room. Alicia grabbed her bag before rushing after him. 'I told you, she is not a liar, Mr D'Aquanni—'

He stopped at the top of the stairs and Alicia cannoned into his back. He turned and gripped her arms, holding her steady when she reeled slightly from coming into contact with his hard, muscle-packed form.

'Enough! I don't want to hear another word about this ridiculous claim. A helicopter will take us to the landing strip in Milan.' He let her go abruptly, as if fearful of catching something from her, and perversely Alicia was stung and at the same time bemused. She'd come for this, had wanted to force him to return and face the music, but now she couldn't quite believe it was happening.

'You…you're going to take me?'

An arctic glance slid up and down her body. 'With a one-way ticket here and barely enough money for a meal, not to mention a credit card I can only imagine is already maxed out, I don't imagine you'd get very far in a hurry.' *And this has to be cleared up*.

He walked away from her down the wide stairs, a harsh inflection in his voice as it floated back up. 'You and your sister picked the wrong man to play games with, Miss Parker. I am not going to entertain any further discussion about this *baby*. I will not be held to ransom by some half-baked accusation of parenthood.' He turned and looked up darkly from the bottom of the stairs. 'And you are not going to leave my sight until this is concluded to my satisfaction. You will pay for having so sorely tested my patience.'

Alicia stood still for a moment when he turned and walked away and then thought a little hysterically that at least she wouldn't have to worry about how she was going to get home. He was right. With only a questionable amount of credit left on her card, she really hadn't even thought that far ahead, to her return. Her driving concern had been to see Dante D'Aquanni.

And now she had. As she followed him down the stairs she felt very queasily as if she were on a train and they had just changed track for some unknown and very scary destination. And she knew, with that sick feeling, that there was no way she could call a halt and get off.

Dante glanced across the aisle of his plane. The woman's face was averted, her body tense and huddled into the seat, which seemed to dwarf her petite form. She was staring out of the window at the white expanse of cloud as if it contained some fascinating image that he couldn't see. He wanted to go over, haul her out of the seat and demand payment for disrupting his life, making him trek all the way back to England, which had laid claim to him for almost a year previously. Make her pay— *how?* asked a snide voice as an unwelcome image of her crushed into his arms, her head falling back, throat and mouth bared for his kisses, inserted itself like a lurid B movie image into his imagination.

His face hardened. She'd been silent since leaving the house. She'd shown no awe or surprise at the experience of being taken by helicopter to the private landing strip of a tiny airport reserved only for VIPs and dignitaries. When they had been in the helicopter she had not even needed to be told what to do, what safety procedures to follow. She'd done them automatically.

So she was accustomed to the luxury that private helicopter travel afforded. While it didn't gel immediately with the downbeat image she portrayed—he could vaguely remember jeans and another shapeless dark top in London, her hair tied back—he had to concede that she'd quickly smashed his first impressions. She'd proven that, with just soap and water; a lily had lain underneath all the grime and dust, under the voluminous garments. His chest tightened at the thought of how much a little more gilding might make her even more alluring. How the silk of a custom-made dress would skim and cling enticingly to those slight curves…

Alicia turned her head as though compelled and found Dante looking at her with an intense expression on his face. It made more than a quiver of awareness run through her. It made her heart flip and thump unevenly.

He settled back into his seat and regarded her coolly. She couldn't look away and she felt a flush come up under her skin.

Contradicting his own avowal not to mention it, he asked, 'Tell me why you are so certain that I am the father of your sister's baby.'

Alicia fought to stay calm. She couldn't believe he was being so obtuse, and then she felt slightly sick. Perhaps the man did have so many lovers that he literally didn't know one from the other. And yet…he seemed far too discriminating for that kind of behaviour which led her again to wonder what he had seen in Melanie.

'Because,' she bit out, 'she told me and I trust her. She's my sister.' Something made her defiant then. 'You're not making this trip for the good of your health so you obviously believe me, even if you say you don't.'

His jaw clenched and he leant forward slightly, even though a few feet separated them. Alicia leant back into her seat. 'What did she say exactly?'

Alicia took a calming breath. 'I asked her who had done this to her. She said you, how she'd been on her way to try and see you when the accident happened…how you'd sent her away. I knew she was seeing someone from work, I just had no idea it was you.'

He frowned slightly. 'To the best of my knowledge, she was still working for me.'

'Yes…but she obviously meant you sent her away from her association with you. She was still feverish, in shock. She'd just suffered a major accident.' Alicia could feel the shock setting in again.

Dante shook his head incredulously as something became very clear to him. He cursed himself for not having seen it before. 'Your sister would know that the merger is coming up. She knows how vulnerable I am to public scandal at this moment...' He shook his head. 'I know *exactly* what you and she are up to now.'

Alicia leant forward again, her hands clenched, her eyes bright. 'Signore D'Aquanni, right now she is fighting for her life, she's not up to anything beyond that. And as for me, do you really think I've nothing better to do than chase around Europe trying to get some holier-than-thou autocratic billionaire playboy to speak to me?'

He looked at her coolly and then said, 'You can drop the act now, it's unnecessary.' He turned away from her, making her insides boil over with fury.

She undid her belt and stood up from the seat, her face pink with rage. His calculating dismissive look had driven her blood pressure even higher. As if he knew something she didn't. He looked back up at her as she planted herself in front of him, hands on hips.

'You really are unbelievable. Do you think you're so untouchable that you can treat people like things? Like...' she flung her hand out '...toys to be played with and then discarded when you're bored? You might have grown up getting your own way, but that's not how—'

In that instant the plane suddenly hit some turbulence and Alicia was thrown forward and off balance. With deadly inevitability and in sickening slow motion, she fell straight into Dante D'Aquanni's lap.

The wind was knocked out of her and she was plastered against his front. And when she tried to move, hard arms held her captive. In a second she became aware of hard, taut thigh muscles under her bottom, a very hard chest and his breath, feathering across her face. He smelt fresh, masculine, musky.

She struggled in earnest, in panic at the way her own body was responding eagerly. 'Let me go.'

'No way. I'm far too interested in hearing the end of your tirade. Please, do go on. I believe you were about to tell me how things work.' His voice was innocuous enough, not a hint of the extreme torture of her squirming position on his lap.

She looked up and wished she hadn't. His face, that mouth, was inches away and his eyes told the real story of the emotion behind his words. They were dark and utterly cold. Remote.

'I...I...' Her voice sounded squeaky, ineffectual. Why, oh, why, did she have to be so aware of him physically? He was the enemy, the man who had rejected her sister, who even now was denying paternity. This man was the lowest of the low...

'Actually, I'm not interested in what you have to say, as you're so far from the truth it's not even funny. What I am interested in, however, is this...'

And, before Alicia could ask what he meant, his mouth had landed on hers and she was transported back in time to the previous evening. Every nerve ending exploded into a tiny ball of fire. It was madness, insanity, this instantaneous effect he had.

One of his hands had found its way underneath her sweater and was climbing up over her skin, skimming her waist. Her breasts throbbed as if on cue and swelled to tight points. She wriggled as a shaft of pure arousal pulsed between her legs and Dante groaned softly against her mouth. Her heart thumped even faster, reality slipping away with an inexorability that Alicia couldn't fight.

His hand cupped one of her breasts and, with aching slowness, his thumb found and rubbed against the tight bud under its covering of lace. *Hard, not soft,* went through her overheated brain as the callused feel of his hands were an exquisite torture against her sensitive skin. Alicia's head fell back, her eyes closed. She'd never, ever felt like this before—this immediate fire that erupted and washed away any resistance. The only time she'd come close to anything like this—

Her thoughts seized to an icy halt as a memory surfaced and she stiffened. Dante's hand was seeking her other breast and Alicia was aghast to see that she'd shifted in order to offer him easier access. She seized on that painful memory and pushed with all her might against him. His arms loosened and she tumbled back and out of the seat, landing on her rear on the soft carpet.

What the hell had just happened?

She stood awkwardly, breathing heavily. She wiped the back of her hand across her mouth, her eyes huge. She dropped her hand and her mouth was pink, her cheeks glowing red. Dante said nothing, his face implacable, barely a hair out of place. Unmoved.

'Don't touch me ever again. You make me sick.'

And, before he could see how much turmoil she was in, she turned and fled to the toilet at the front of the cabin, narrowly avoiding the stewardess, who appeared just then with a tray piled high with food and drinks.

After spending an inordinately long time in the bathroom splashing cold water on her face and wrists, Alicia emerged. She wondered what kind of spell this man held over her and felt sick to the stomach at the thought of facing Melanie when she'd proven herself to be no less immune to his *charms*. For a brief cataclysmic moment in there, faced with her own bewildered image, she'd actually wished that somehow he wasn't the father of Melanie's baby. She was going to be the aunt of this man's child, for goodness' sake. Her stomach had lurched ominously and she thought for a second that she'd be sick.

But when she emerged, steeled to see him again, the cabin was empty. The stewardess turned around from where she'd been laying out cutlery and plates. Alicia thought hysterically that Dante must have parachuted out in order to get away from her. The cool blonde woman cut through her thoughts. 'Mr D'Aquanni has taken a call in the office at the back of the plane. He said to call me if you need anything. We'll be landing in a little under an hour, Ms Parker.'

Alicia nodded. She couldn't trust herself to speak. Of course the plane had an office. Silly her, she chided herself. And no doubt he was as disgusted by what had just happened as she was. Her cheeks burned as she recalled what it must have looked like. She had practically thrown herself into his arms, had all but begged him to keep going…

Dante sat at the back of the plane, his call having lasted only a couple of minutes. His body still hummed, his trousers still felt tight. He'd watched, uncharacteristically speechless as Alicia had walked into the bathroom. When she'd landed on his lap, in his mind's eye he'd seen very clearly what he should do—put her away from him and back to her own seat. But his arms had come around her instinctively. His lap had cupped her bottom as if it had known it from a previous existence. And the feel of her tiny, curved form had been so seductive that he'd found it nigh on impossible to remember the rage that her words had sparked within him.

But without her bewitching presence he could remember. How dared she presume to know what kind of upbringing he'd had? It had been more like an up-dragging. He'd fought and kicked every step of the way, staying on the right side of the law only by the mercy of some divine force. And if it hadn't been for Stefano Arrigi plucking him and his brother from the streets when he had, who knew where he—*they*—might have ended up…?

He cursed the woman for making him think of these things. He knew rationally that he couldn't entirely blame her as he'd never publicized his background—oh, the information was there, he couldn't move without someone commenting on it—but he'd learnt the hard way that once you had money people didn't much care how you'd got it, and yet Alicia's condemnation had cut him in a tender place. And he had no idea why. She was a complete stranger to him.

He didn't seek pity from anyone. Especially when he had

such a bitter memory of the one and only time he *had* told someone the truth—a woman. And yet he felt instinctively that *this* woman would somehow empathise. Or, more accurately, *pretend* to.

He stood abruptly, making some papers fall from the desk. The sooner they got to England and sorted this farce out the better. And the sooner he made sure this woman had no recourse or claim, however bogus, on his life, the better. He vowed that within the day he would be back in his villa on Lake Como, any threat from these women nullified and eradicated.

Dante returned to the main cabin just as the plane was landing and Alicia studiously avoided looking anywhere near him. She trembled inside. Watching the ground below become clearer and clearer, she could make out fields, buildings, tiny cars…she realized then that she hadn't told him where to go but they were in fact circling over the Oxford area.

She turned around. 'How did you know where to come? I never told you.'

She was relieved to see him buttoned up, suit jacket on.

'I know because it didn't take much to find out.'

Alicia had to consciously stop her gaze from dropping to his mouth, the strong brown column of his throat. 'Oh…'

'You never did tell me what you want the money for exactly, or how much… You pulled your fainting stunt just before you did. Which was, no doubt, designed somewhat crudely to arouse sympathy.' His tone was conversational, bored even.

Alicia's heart hardened. The man was a bastard. She hated him. He had hurt Melanie unforgivably.

She tried to keep her voice steady but it was a struggle. Briefly, she told him of Melanie's injuries. 'She's going to need the expert ongoing care of one of the best gynaecologists in the UK who specializes in post trauma cases, and he is only available privately. Even if we had the money, he's based in central London, so we would have to move closer in order to see him once a week. Melanie won't be able to withstand a lengthy public transport journey. He works in Harley Street. You do the maths.' She flung the last words at him in a fit of pique at his lack of expression. Tears stung her eyes again. Damn it, if Melanie or the baby suffered because of this man… She turned away in despair. She wouldn't be surprised if when they landed he threw her from the plane and closed the door only to take off, back to Italy.

Dante watched the slim column of her throat work in profile. Was she really upset or was this part of the game? *As if he had to ask.* He had thought for a brief moment of seeing her out of the plane door, closing it behind her and taking off immediately. But he knew he couldn't. Melanie Parker was a reality. She *was* associated with him. It would be an easy story to sell and he was damned if he'd let her.

He focused on his recent conversation with his assistant in Italy. They were still unable to track down his younger brother. His mouth tightened. If this pregnancy was genuine, Paolo D'Aquanni had a lot to answer for.

CHAPTER FOUR

'YOUR sister has been conscious for a few hours now. We're cautiously optimistic that she's not going to lapse again.'

Alicia felt weak with relief. 'And the baby?'

The ward sister nodded. 'The baby is doing fine.' She shook her head incredulously. 'It's a miracle really how it survived the impact of the crash but, as you know, this is only the first step. She's going to need constant care to ensure its healthy progress. It's such a relief that Paolo has managed to make the first appointment for Mel to see Dr Hardy in London in a couple of weeks. I was afraid it'd be too short notice.'

Alicia's back tensed; she felt Dante straighten beside her. She struggled to interpret the words she'd just heard. 'What are you talking about? Who is Paolo?'

Her friend gave her a funny look. 'Why, Mel's boyfriend, of course, silly. He arrived last night. He stayed in the chair beside her bed, absolutely besotted.' She bustled towards the ward, guiding them in. 'She's still very weak, so maybe don't make it a long visit today, OK?'

Alicia felt herself nod dumbly. She still couldn't process the words. She was vaguely aware of Dante behind her, his hand moving to her back, propelling her forward. She moved, but didn't know how. They were in a ward of four beds, the curtains pulled around her sister's. Somehow instinctively Alicia just *knew* that everything was about to fall apart.

And when she pulled back the curtain she nearly fainted for the second time in two days.

'Lissy...' Melanie's weakened voice was a thread of its normal chatty vitality but Alicia couldn't even look at her yet. She couldn't move. She stared in abject mounting horror at a younger, slightly less good looking, slightly smaller version of Dante D'Aquanni. She had to be so exhausted that she was hallucinating. That was it—extreme tiredness and stress... She raised a hand to her head.

'Lissy? Are you OK?'

Finally she turned to look at her sister and blanched when she saw her still too pale face, one livid scar still across her forehead. But a hint of colour warmed her cheeks under the sickly pallor and the sight of her bump under the bedclothes was reassuring. Alicia nodded her head jerkily.

An autocratic hand propelled her towards a chair beside the bed. Melanie reached out a hand and took Alicia's in hers. 'What is it? The nurses said you'd been gone since yesterday... Where did you—'

Melanie broke off and looked from Alicia to Dante D'Aquanni, who she'd just noticed. Out of the corner of her eye, Alicia saw the younger man stand, bristling.

Melanie's voice sounded strained and Alicia could see this man take her hand in support. 'Mr D'Aquanni... What are you doing here?'

Dante stepped forward into the light and seemed to Alicia to energise the small space. 'Your sister here seems to be under the misapprehension that I am the father of your unborn child.' Alicia couldn't be unaware of the way his glance flicked down to the bump of her sister's belly, as if to confirm for himself that she had been telling the truth.

Melanie looked at Alicia. 'How…what…however did you get that idea?'

Alicia fought valiantly against sinking into the ground into the comfort of another dead faint. She couldn't look at Dante.

'When I came here last week, you were feverish…I asked you who had done this to you and all you said was, "Dante D'Aquanni," his was the only name you mentioned… You said you'd been on your way to see him. You asked me to find him for you…'

'I did?'

Alicia smiled sadly. This wasn't Melanie's fault. 'You probably don't remember.'

Melanie groaned and glanced at the young man beside her shyly. 'I *had* been on my way to see Mr D'Aquanni.' She glanced at him then with a little trepidation. 'But it was only to ask him to bring back Paolo…'

'Paolo…' Alicia repeated dumbly.

Dante spoke then, and Alicia flinched slightly at the harshness of his tone. 'Paolo D'Aquanni—the man your sister was having an affair with at the office. My *brother.*'

His words seemed to come from far away. Alicia looked across at Paolo. 'So you're…'

Melanie squeezed her hand. 'Yes, Lissy, he's the one, the father of my baby.'

Distaste flavoured Dante's mouth. His eyes raked over Melanie, taking in her undoubtedly weakened state. He had to admit that she couldn't have faked the crash. She looked to be taller than Alicia; they shared the same colouring, but her eyes were blue, not a deep, dark chocolate brown. He ruthlessly drove down his awareness of the small woman beside the bed.

This touching scene left him cold. *These two women* held such echoes of the past for him that he wanted to stop this charade at once. And yet his brother was looking at Melanie with such naked love and already, sickeningly, Dante knew the damage had been done. These women were wily operators, reacting to the changing circumstances, the arrival of Paolo, with sheer bold bravado. He was quite certain that the baby was no more Paolo's than his…and Paolo was naive and silly enough to believe it.

History was being repeated…

Dante bit out curtly, 'Paolo, I'd like to talk to you for a moment privately.'

The young man coloured and swallowed, but he followed his older brother out. Alicia felt a little sorry for him but sagged back with relief when they had left. The shock still reverberated through her body, numbing her to her churning stomach and brain.

Alicia knew instinctively from that short moment between the brothers that Dante was the supreme boss and she, in spectacular style, had no doubt blasted any sympathy Dante might have had for Paolo and this situation… What a mess. And it was entirely her fault. She focused on her sister. She couldn't worry Melanie.

Quashing the looming worries—the thought of what Dante might do and feelings of intense guilt—Alicia got up to give her sister a quick hug and kiss. She was OK, that was the main thing.

'Oh, Mel…' tears threatened '…I thought I'd lost you.'

Melanie's eyes filled too. 'Don't, Lissy. I'm not going anywhere. Especially not now that Paolo is here.' Her cheeks did flood with colour then and, as glad as Alicia was to see it, she knew she had to be careful not to let her get overexcited. 'Oh, Lissy, we're going to get married! He's asked me to marry him. And we're going to move into town so I can be near Dr Hardy—'

Alicia looked at Melanie seriously, knowing that they were still not certain of anything. 'Melanie…'

Melanie shook her head emphatically. '*He's* the one—the one I couldn't mention. When Mr D'Aquanni found out about us seeing each other he went beserk. He sent Paolo to the office in Tokyo. But we kept in touch. Then, a couple of months after he left, I found out I was pregnant. I'd been so upset about him being sent away that I hadn't even noticed my periods stopping.' She looked at Alicia sheepishly. 'I had been planning on going out there too. I didn't care if I'd have to leave the company, just so we could be together but then...' she looked at her belly fondly for a second... 'I couldn't go. I want to have my baby here. I was going to beg Mr D'Aquanni to let him come back.'

Alicia looked at her and shook her head. 'Why didn't you tell me?'

Melanie sighed. 'I couldn't, Lissy. I tried calling the camp but couldn't get through. I didn't want to send it in an e-mail as you might have been worried...and I'd got your e-mail to say you were due home soon anyway. I wanted it to be a nice surprise, for me and Paolo to be together when you met him for the first time...'

Alicia smoothed back some hair from her sister's forehead. 'Oh, hon...'

At that moment the two men came back into the small cubicle. Dante looked dangerous. Paolo came back to Melanie's side and took her hand again, staring at his brother belligerently.

Dante wasn't happy. His expression was stony and remote. He looked at Alicia. 'I'll give you a lift home now.'

'But I've just got here.'

'Alicia...'

Something stopped her immediate retort. His voice seemed to act like some kind of hypnotic beacon to her weakened body and mind. She wasn't ready to be alone with this man, to face the obvious recriminations coming her way, and yet...it seemed like the only thing she could do was to answer his summons.

She looked at Melanie and her younger sister suddenly seemed like the one in control, frail though she was. 'You *should* go, Lissy, get some sleep. You haven't had a moment's rest since you came home…'

As Alicia hovered between getting up and staying where she was, Melanie pulled her towards her at the last second and whispered into her ear, clasping her hand, 'Liss, you don't have to worry about me any more; I have Paolo now.'

Alicia stood and swayed ominously. She felt as though she were on a dinghy that had been cut loose from the shore and was floating helplessly out to sea, everything she knew becoming a smaller and smaller dot in the distance. And, to compound this feeling, Dante was immediately there, his arm around her an unwelcome support. She tried to ignore its effect, looked across at Paolo and smiled weakly. 'It was nice to meet you.'

He nodded soberly. 'You, too.' He promptly turned his attention back to Melanie.

And then she was walking away, with Dante's arm still around her. It was only when they reached the main entrance of the hospital and the cool air rushed forward and embraced her that Alicia found the strength to pull away jerkily. Too much had just happened for her to process fully and her insides clawed with shame and guilt at how badly she'd misconstrued things.

She looked at Dante with her arms wrapped tight around her body. So many emotions were rushing through her that she didn't even know where to start. She felt herself being pulled in a million different directions and a very scary feeling of relief, which she hadn't had the courage to acknowledge yet because it wasn't entirely to do with Melanie's recovery.

Bravely she stuck her chin out, looking at Dante directly. 'I'm sorry.'

Dante looked at her for a long moment and she had to fight not to look away from his penetrating gaze. He looked like an exotic Italian prince against the backdrop of the grey English hospital. A group of nurses passed and stared openly at him, their appreciation obvious as they went through the doors. He didn't seem to notice. His expression was blank. Scarily blank. After what seemed like an age, he said simply, quietly, 'Sorry?'

Something in his manner made the past rear its ugly head. Alicia could remember all too well what it had been like to see a foreign god on domestic soil. She had been one of those nurses in the not too distant past and, even though she knew it was irrational, that he was a different person, that it was projection, an ugly emotion rose up.

She felt it rise and welcomed it. 'Yes. Sorry.' She waved an airy hand, not knowing where this ability to act so nonchalantly had come from. A part of her was completely aghast at what she'd hurled at this man by way of insult and accusation—all unfounded. But…something else was driving her.

'I had very good reason for believing that you *were* the father of my sister's baby. I'd just got off a long flight, had come home to find my sister in hospital, *five months pregnant,* apparently abandoned by the father. I had no idea who her lover was and the only name she mentioned then was yours… She was in need of expensive medical care… How do you think I came to the conclusions I did, given how I felt?'

Dante regarded her. She was priceless. She couldn't even be bothered to act contrite, now that she was sure that they had at least one D'Aquanni falling for their plan. His mouth quirked. 'Oh, I think I have an idea.'

Immediately she felt deflated and humbled. Seeing his brother there must have been a shock to him, although, since he'd known of the relationship, slightly less than hers. Something niggled at her then but she couldn't hold on to it, still too stunned… 'Of course you do; I'm sorry.'

'That's three "I'm sorry"s—how many more do you think will make up for the chaos you've brought into my life?' *And the chaos you're no doubt still planning on bringing into our lives…*

Alicia stood as tall as she could. 'I'm sorry, I'm sorry, I'm sorry. There. Believe me, I'm truly sorry I ever believed you to be the father, that I went all the way to your offices, to your villa…' She had become more and more worked up with her words, the shock wearing off and felt herself starting to dissolve. She stepped back and away, her throat thick with tears. She just had to get away from him—*now.* 'Just…I'm sorry, OK? I'll get a bus home, you can go back to Italy on your plane and forget we ever met. Forget about the money. Melanie and I will look after ourselves.' *After all, we've been doing it all our lives…*

Dante had to fight the urge to roll his eyes and say, Oh, please. Now she was going to the other extreme and starting to seriously overact.

Alicia couldn't think clearly, she was too consumed with the shock after shock, too used to thinking of herself and Melanie as a self-contained unit. Her head was churning so much that she couldn't process the information calmly, see the way forward. To see that they did have another person who had pledged to help—Paolo. She just needed to get away from Dante right now, her emotions were raw and too near the surface. He was too…too much.

She turned and started to walk away, the car park in front of her a blur through her swimming eyes. God. She hadn't cried in years, despite some of the scenes she'd witnessed in Africa, and here she was, blubbing every two minutes. And fainting like some wan heroine from a bad costume drama.

A hard hand caught her arm, swinging her back. All she could see was a huge, dark blurry shape. She couldn't speak. The next thing she knew, she was wrapped in arms so strong and so comforting that she would have believed it if she'd been told at that moment that she was in heaven. She cried for what seemed like an aeon. For herself. For Melanie.

And for accusing this man wrongly, for not being able to say sorry with any grace because he was causing all manner of scary feelings in her belly. The tears came until her eyes were dry and her throat was raw.

* * *

Despite his best intentions, Dante had reacted on pure impulse and an instinct so strong that he'd had no alternative but to let it run through him. He knew her tears were part of the act—*knew it*. But something in her body as she'd turned away had made him pull her back, unable to let her walk away.

He'd never held a crying woman in his arms before.

Physical desire.

That was all it was. He couldn't fathom it, couldn't rationalize it—it just *was*. Something about this woman was calling to him on a base level and he knew he had to see it through to its conclusion. No matter what it took. With customary ruthlessness that made him feel on safer ground, he started to formulate a plan of sorts. It would placate Paolo, who was proving to be dismayingly, resolutely obstinate in his support of Melanie, and it would mean he could keep an eye on Alicia *and her sister*. And he would get her into his bed to sate this burning fire…

Her body had finally stopped its uncontrollable shaking. He could feel her take a deep breath against his chest, and her soft breasts rise and swell against his belly. His groin tightened, the blood rushed south. He was making the right decision. He pulled away, tipping her head back to face him with one hand, almost hoping for a second that she'd have turned into some kind of hag in the interim, like in a cartoon.

But no…she looked exquisite. Her eyes were huge, the colour of crushed dark velvet and dewed with moisture, her mouth a quivering invitation, the tracks of tears on her cheeks an enticement to drop his head, kiss them away…

He saw something in her eyes then, a vulnerability that she hadn't displayed before…*because she'd been too busy being brave*… The thought sneaked in and stunned him with its rogue audacity for a second. For that second, before his cynical brain could kick into gear again, he was caught by something else.

With his thumb he gently touched the healing cut on her

cheek. She flinched ever so slightly and then shock slammed into him. Everything jumped back into sharp focus.

What was he doing? Thinking?

He was no better than his poor duped brother at that moment. He felt the need to pull back. Retreat. He was fast heading into uncharted waters and didn't like it. The woman and her sister were consummate actresses and manipulators—nothing had changed that fact—and yet here he was, letting himself be swayed by a few crocodile tears.

'Let's get you home.' He put her away from him and made a quick curt call on his mobile. Within seconds the sleek black car that had taken them from the plane to the hospital slid to a silent halt beside them. Alicia trembled slightly and felt an awful shiver of foreboding skate down her spine when she saw how Dante's face had turned back into a mask of cool indifference. For one moment there, she could have sworn she'd seen something else, something far more *human*.

He stopped her just before she got into the car. She looked up warily.

'Just for the record, don't let Paolo's fervent avowal to marry Melanie and look after her lull you into complacency that your plan has worked. I'm still under no illusions that Paolo is about as likely to be the father as myself.'

Alicia's jaw clenched hard and before she could articulate a word she was being unceremoniously handed into the back of the car, one thought in her head: *he's not human at all; he's cold and cruel...*

CHAPTER FIVE

'HAVE you seen it?'

'I'm looking at it right now.' Dante was grim. With one hand he held his mobile to his ear, with the other he held open the front of the tabloid. Breakfast sat uneaten at his hotel room table. It was the following morning and he was still here in England. That uncomfortable fact was not lost on Dante. He flicked the paper again to see the picture more clearly and stretched long legs out.

His assistant sounded mildly exasperated, and only the fact that they went back so far gave him the audacity to say, 'Well? Care to tell me what it's about?'

'Not particularly, Alex.' *Because, in truth, he still wasn't even sure himself what had happened...*

A sigh came down the other end of the phone. 'Look, Dante, there's a photo of you kissing a strange woman on the steps of your villa, very passionately I might add. The merger conference is days away. The Americans have made a big deal about no unnecessary publicity. You *know* Buchanen has always disapproved of your playboy status…and with his strategic importance—'

'I am aware of that Alex.' Dante bit out. 'And I'm two steps ahead of you. The woman is called Alicia Parker and she will be accompanying me to the conference as my…' he searched for the right word… 'hostess.'

'Oh…' His assistant was momentarily lost for words. He wasn't even going to bother attempting to ask where she'd emerged from, knowing he'd be stonewalled. 'Is she aware of this?'

'Not yet. But it won't be a problem.' Dante terminated the call and smiled but it was a shark's smile. This photographer, who'd had his camera confiscated but who had somehow managed to take a snap anyway, had played beautifully into his hands. He made a phone call.

'Paolo? Come and see me at the hotel please.'

Alicia woke and felt strange. Curiously rested. For a second she was totally disorientated. And then she realized that she was in her old room. In the apartment she'd shared with Melanie before going to Africa. Realising where she was sent sudden panic rushing through her. Melanie! And then she sagged back against the mattress. *All* the events came rushing back. And with them, Dante D'Aquanni. He had brought her here yesterday and left her at the door. They'd said a stilted goodbye. Well, she thought slightly defensively to herself, what could she say to a man whose life she'd single-handedly upended? To a man who still believed himself and his brother to be victims of a huge scam, orchestrated by her and her sister. Alicia could have laughed if it wasn't so ridiculous. Melanie was so scatty she barely had the wherewithal to make it to work in the morning, never mind dream up such an elaborate scheme…

The fact was, Dante was *not* the father of Melanie's baby. His brother was. And if their greeting had been anything to go by, quite apart from his own assertion to her, he most certainly wouldn't be bankrolling his brother's *love affair,* baby or no.

Dante D'Aquanni was not going to play the part of benevolent uncle.

So she was back to square one. Feeling a little resurgence of her old energy as she got up, Alicia was thankful. She was going to need it. Even if they could at least count on Paolo's promise, his wages, she would have to work hard now too, to try and finance moving them to London and guaranteeing Dr Hardy's care for Melanie. She couldn't even contemplate not getting her that care. Melanie was everything to her. Her whole world. Ever since they'd been dropped at the steps of the orphanage by their sick, harried and stressed mother. Alicia had been four, Melanie two and half. Alicia had held tight on to Melanie's hand as she'd wailed uncontrollably. She could still remember the stoic calm she'd felt watching her mother's thin back as she walked away. She hadn't looked back once. And Alicia hadn't seen her since.

She blanked those thoughts. She didn't have time for sad memories. She made a quick call to the hospital. Melanie was getting better and better and sounded strong. *And* distracted—Paolo was still with her. Alicia put down the phone with a frown. She wasn't sure how she felt about Paolo, if they could trust him, although he seemed to be genuine and certainly didn't seem to share his brother's dark, suspicious nature. She shouldn't have stayed away for so long; she would have met him before now if she'd been at home.

But she hadn't been able to leave, she'd been sucked into the relentless grind of trying to save so many lives.

But she was home now. That was what mattered. Tying her hair back with a band, she was walking towards the bathroom when a knock sounded on the door just feet away. Immediately and for no good reason, Alicia's heart started to pound. She glanced quickly down at herself—faded loose pyjama bottoms, an old threadbare sweatshirt. She was presentable enough for the postman or a neighbour.

But it was neither when she opened the door. It was Dante D'Aquanni, the man she'd imagined to be firmly ensconsed back in his palatial, idyllic villa, no doubt thankful to have her out of his hair.

She blinked up at him. He looked gorgeous and devastating in another dark suit. 'You...'

'Yes. Me.' His glance flickered down her body and her bare feet curled into the carpet.

'What are you doing here? Why aren't you gone?' Her hand gripped the door.

'Aren't you going to ask me in?'

What choice did she have? She moved back to allow him through and the sheer size of him as he passed her made her legs feel weak. He even had to duck his head. The apartment was like a doll's house with him in it.

She closed the door. He was looking around, taking in the bare furnishings, the photos of the smiling sisters, a few books on the shelves. When he looked at Alicia he could see something flare in her eyes and her chin tilt up defiantly. He recognized that look because he'd seen it before—on *himself*. It was a look that said, We may not have much but it's ours...mine. The immediate empathy he felt surprised him; he covered it up. And also covered up the way her sleep-flushed face made him want to reach out...touch her cheek. Touch more than her cheek.

Alicia tried to remain calm, not to allow the tremor she felt develop into uncontrollable shaking. He was obviously just here to reiterate that she and Melanie would be getting nothing. To make sure she didn't go to the papers. To tell her to keep her sister away from Paolo. And right then, despite her recent misgivings, she vowed that if he did, she'd fight him tooth and nail. Because even if *he* wasn't the father, Paolo, his brother was, whether he chose to believe it or not. She was prepared to accept that Dante wouldn't pay, but he couldn't separate Paolo and Melanie now. And, assuming he'd meant the marriage proposal, Melanie would need Paolo's support desperately, although she'd have to leave that to Melanie to discuss with him…Alicia's head started to pound. Why did everything have to be so complicated?

Dante slid his gaze up and down. It turned mocking.

'Don't you own one fitted garment with its colours still intact?'

Stung, and hating herself for it because she didn't normally give two hoots about her appearance, Alicia asked sweetly, 'What? Haven't you heard that the messy-chic look is in?' She cocked her hip and gestured with a hand. 'If you open the magazines they're all wearing these clothes.'

Then pride made her straighten her spine. 'There isn't much call for high fashion among the refugee tents in Africa, Signore D'Aquanni. But, as I doubt we're ever likely to move in the same circles, you shouldn't have to endure my wardrobe insulting your sensibilities. Now, I'm sure you haven't lowered yourself to come here to discuss my lack of style.'

His eyes narrowed on her for a long moment. 'So you did work in Africa then?'

Alicia tensed so much she thought she might break. 'Yes. For a year.'

He passed a look over her that patently said he put her claim under serious doubt and then, to her surprise, he took off his jacket and sat down on the couch. It was a three-seater but he practically took up the whole thing.

'Actually, Alicia, your style or lack of it is one of the things that will come up for discussion. Now, what does a man have to do to be offered coffee around here?'

Alicia cupped her mug of steaming coffee in her hands and looked at Dante warily over the rim. She perversely hoped that he was sitting on the bit of sofa with the exposed spring. But, looking completely at ease, unconcerned, Dante sipped his own coffee, taking his time before setting the cup down on the low table. He leant forward and rested his arms on his knees.

'I'm here to offer you a proposal.'

Alicia could feel the blood drain from her face and then rush back guiltily as she realized what she'd taken his words to mean for a split second. He'd seen it too and that mocking look made his mouth quirk at the corner again.

'Not that kind of proposal. *Never* that kind of proposal; I'm not a marrying man.'

Words were strangled in her throat. She was mortified that he would think that she had thought he'd meant marriage. *And she had.* For a second.

She put her cup down with a shaky hand. 'Look, just tell me why you're here, I have things to do.' She sat back and folded her arms across her chest and glared at him. He settled back into the couch and crossed one leg over the other. The bottom of his impeccably shod foot seemed to mock her too. She could see how in some cultures it was taken as a high insult to be faced with the soles of someone's feet.

'What I've come here to *propose* is a little mutual arrangement.'

Alicia all but snorted. She doubted very much that this man did anything *mutually*.

'I'm listening.'

Only so you'll be gone more quickly and I can get back to normal and forget we ever met.

Alicia conveniently blocked out the voice that said, What about if Melanie and Paolo get married? What about when they have the baby? Won't Uncle Dante come to visit? Won't Uncle Dante be there for the rest of your life?

His voice cut through her tortured thoughts. 'I am hosting a series of final negotiations in a very high profile merger over the next three weeks. The first week of the conference will be at my villa in Lake Como—a week in which the very select participants will be shielded from the media's prying eyes, to be exclusively wined and dined in between meetings.'

Alicia looked at him blankly, desperately trying to hide the effect his force field had on her body. She just hoped he'd hurry up and say whatever he had to say, not knowing why he felt he had to tell her anything…

'Together with a close colleague from Ireland, we're merging forces with one of the biggest construction giants in America. As I am the biggest investor, effectively it is a merger that will see me as CEO of the largest construction conglomerate in the world.'

Alicia recalled Melanie's glowing comments when she had first got the job at Dante's company some years previously. 'I thought you already were the biggest company in the world…' She couldn't keep the caustic tone from her voice, or the look in her eye that told him exactly what she thought of his obvious bid for world domination.

He ignored her effortlessly and said without any emotion, just as a hard fact, 'I am; however, there's always room for improvement.'

'You mean greed,' Alicia muttered, and felt pettish as she did so. What did she care, even if he wanted to conquer outer space?

Again he ignored her barbed comments. 'The construction company from America is run by a man called Buchanen. He's taken a lot of persuading to come on board. Years of smaller negotiations have led us to this point, and now we are poised to sign on the dotted line. All it's going to take is this three weeks and then it's going to be signed, sealed and delivered.'

Satisfaction rushed through Dante. *This would be the pinnacle of everything he'd ever set out to achieve, to prove… having come from nothing…*and he was not about to let that satisfaction be thwarted. Especially when so many depended on him.

He lay an arm along the back of the couch, making his shirt strain across his impossibly broad and hard chest, making Alicia's eyes drop betrayingly and her throat dry up. She looked up and felt a rising tide of red. And saw the mocking look in his eye. At that moment she wanted to throw the contents of her coffee cup in his face.

'*And…?* I presume there's more?' she bit out.

Dante regarded her, taking in every expression crossing her face, flashing through her big eyes. His groin tightened. *You bet there is…*

He schooled his expression, veiled the lust he felt. 'Buchanen has been a reluctant investor. And yet he's the only one we want. He controls just *one* of the biggest companies in the US, but he's got the most links and connections with Europe, which will inevitably give us an even stronger hold here too. But he's cautious. He's planning to run for the American senate and that's pretty much the reason he finally gave in; he wants to free up his time to devote himself to politics—the downside of that is his concern for his untarnished reputation.'

Alicia was beginning to feel more than a little confused. And more and more hot and bothered. 'Yes, but what does all this have to do with me?'

Dante said nothing and reached into his jacket pocket to pull out a folded newspaper. Alicia immediately recognized the red top of the tabloid. Her stomach fell. This could only mean one thing. Dante leaned across and put the paper down in front of her. It took a minute for the picture and headline to sink in.

Who is the mysterious woman lighting Dante's inferno?

Even though this was exactly what she'd set out to orchestrate, albeit not with her involvement to such a degree, the reality was shocking, invasive, *awful.* It also made a dark memory surface uncomfortably.

'Oh, my god,' she finally breathed.

'My thoughts entirely. The photographer must have had a smaller digital camera because my security guard confiscated his other one.'

Alicia lifted stricken eyes to Dante. How could she say *sorry* again? She couldn't. She stood up, agitated. She'd rushed off, chasing this man for a crime he hadn't committed and she was no better off for all her efforts. If anything, things were worse.

'I…don't know what to say.' She stood behind her chair, the offending picture still in her eyeline, and all she could remember was the feel of his mouth on hers, his strong, lean, taut body as he'd lifted her off her feet. Her insides liquefied.

He looked up at her steadily and she had a prickling sensation across the back of her neck. She had a feeling that she wasn't going to like what was coming.

'You could do the right thing and say yes when I ask you to come back to Lake Como with me today and be my hostess for the duration of the meetings.'

Alicia's hands gripped the back of the seat. 'I'm…excuse me?'

'I said—'

'I heard you,' she said shakily and came back around the chair to sit down. 'Why on earth would you want me to do that?'

He glanced at the newspaper. 'Because, thanks to your little mercy dash and dramatics, we're now apparently an item.' His mouth twisted with obvious distaste. 'While I've never cared about how I might appear in the media, unfortunately at this moment it is a necessary evil. Buchanen comes from a conservative background; he's a family man and has often made reference to the fact that out of all the particpants, I'm the only one who isn't. In an effort to allay his fears we've encouraged all those involved in the negotiations to bring their families along for the last two weeks if they should so choose.'

A mocking glint lit his dark eyes, making him look rakish and dangerous. 'He's skittish at the moment, very aware of how his every move is being scrutinised. The world's media is watching us with great interest to see if we can pull this merger off, not to mention every other construction consortium in the world… The presence of wives, children will help deflect the heat and hopefully reassure Buchanen.'

In an instant that mocking look had gone and he was coldly

grim. 'If he pulled out, needless to say the merger would be null and void. Millions that have already been invested would be down the drain and no one else would touch us with a barge-pole. As *we're* so inconveniently splashed across the tabloids, you are going to accompany me, be my hostess and put Buchanen's fears of being associated with a playboy to rest.'

He had clearly jumped from asking her to telling her. Alicia was too bewildered to even get angry at his arrogant tone. 'Yes…but even if I did go, wouldn't that almost be worse? I'm not your wife.'

He shook his head and refrained from saying, *No, because I'm never photographed with the same woman twice…* That thought caught him up uncomfortably short for a split second.

'No, because I've never involved a woman in any business dealings before, so he and the press would see this as tantamount to an engagement. The media will bay for my blood if I don't turn up with you now, not to mention what it might do to Buchanen's judgement.'

Alicia gasped, 'You don't expect…'

He smiled and it was cruel. 'Oh I don't think that'll be nec-essary. Your presence will be enough to keep them happy and assure them that I'm not irredeemable. At least until the ink is dry on the contract.'

Alicia twisted her hands in her lap. She'd gone pale. Dante didn't like how her reluctance was making him feel. She looked at him then and that act of vulnerability was back.

'What about that…that woman?' The image of the woman on the steps of the hotel the other night was seared on to her memory, the disparity between them huge to her now and she didn't want him to know she'd seen them. 'The woman the men mentioned…'

Dante frowned for a second and then a look of disdain came over his perfect features. 'She is gone, not in my life.'

Alicia shuddered inwardly at how callously dismissive he was. Panic tinged her voice. 'I can't do it. I couldn't go. I have to stay and take care of Melanie.' Her eyes beseeched him. Surely he wouldn't be that ruthless, that cruel? 'Can't you see? You saw for yourself how weak she is. As it is, I have to go out now and find enough work so that we can pay for her care... If we don't...'

She looked genuinely distraught and it threw Dante for a second. She wasn't looking at him; she'd gone inwards to a place of anxiety that he could only imagine. It had been so long since he'd had to worry about the mundanity of making ends meet, but the sting of it had never faded and he could see it in Alicia now. But he'd anticipated this.

He stood up and leant against the fake fireplace, his hand in his pocket. Alicia looked up and then stood too, hating his easy dominance.

'Signore D'Aquanni, please believe me when I say how sorry I am that I mistook you...and that we've ended up in the papers...'

'You owe me,' he said quietly.

Her head snapped back. 'I *owe* you? Maybe your business meetings should be about human relations, because if you can't see that I need to be with my sick pregnant sister, then—'

'Paolo is going to be with her.'

Alicia stopped in mid-rant. 'What?'

'I said,' Dante said patiently, 'Paolo is going to be with her. My house in London is around the corner from Harley Street. Paolo will stay in London and work in the office here again. He will be five minutes from Melanie's side, and she will be near to all the possible amenities she could need. There is also a housekeeper who will make sure she doesn't have to lift a finger. And a nurse has been arranged for the first month to come daily and make sure Melanie's injuries are healing.'

'But I'm a nurse. If anyone is qualified to look after her it's me—'

He cut in ruthlessly. 'I thought you needed to work. How are you going to work and mind your sister? The nurse I've booked is eminently qualified, specialized in obstetrics and gynaecology.'

Alicia reeled. This was all organized already? She knew Paolo had made the initial appointment, but now this smacked of Dante's involvement. He had upped the ante spectacularly. How could it be this easy? Her vision cleared and she realized just how easy it could be. Her voice was hard and flat, eyes burning.

'And I suppose this dream situation is available to Melanie if I comply with your wish that I should accompany you back to Italy today and play happy families at the conference.'

He shrugged negligently.

'So, in effect, you are blackmailing me, Signore D'Aquanni. You're punishing me, and Melanie.'

He stood then, moving away from the fireplace, and his eyes became dark and hard. Wasn't this exactly what she wanted? '*You* are the one who is responsible for that lurid tabloid splash. And tell me, please, how is providing your sister with the medical care she needs, a luxurious roof over her head, someone to wait on her hand and foot, a punishment? Could you deny her that?'

'Of course not,' Alicia almost wailed, everything in her rebelling against the pull to succumb, to give in. How could she even consider spending a minute more than necessary with this man?

'Look, you don't have to do this. We…*I'll* look after us.' She thought feverishly. 'Now that Paolo is here, he will be supporting Melanie too. We can find somewhere to live and with his wages…'

'*Dio!*' Dante spat out, incensed that she was intent on keeping up this charade of injured innocence. Didn't she know how futile it was? 'Have you really counted the cost of what it would mean to live in the centre of London for up to four months, on top of the medical costs? Do you even know what this man charges?'

Alicia shook her head miserably. She was ashamed to admit that she'd been too scared to check it out properly yet. She'd known it would be astronomical.

He pulled a piece of paper from his pocket and handed it to Alicia. She blanched when she saw the amount; it exceeded even her worst fears. And then it got worse.

'That's just to cover the doctor's basic hourly fee per week for a month. It doesn't even go into any extra kind of care if she might need an operation, not to mention accommodation, food, travel expenses. The mounting costs of a normal pregnancy are considerable, not to mention one that needs constant surveillance.'

Alicia sat down again heavily and Dante sat down too at the end of the couch nearest her.

'Paolo, the little fool, *believes* he is the father of Melanie's baby, wants to play happy families—'

Alicia's face felt like stone; she could feel her blood pressure rise. 'You can believe what you want for now, but the day will come when you will be forced to face the fact that you are wrong.'

He didn't say anything for a moment and then answered grimly, 'Women are adept in the art of obfuscation, manipulation. They were having an affair…he left. She obviously met someone else when he left, then saw her chance.'

'He was sent—' Alicia started to speak furiously but he held up a hand.

'All I'm saying is that I'm prepared to indulge them, for now.'

If it means I get you…

'Paolo has agreed with me to wait until the baby is born and his paternity confirmed before getting married—that's if they still want to. Until that time they can consider themselves engaged and will have the chance to get used to living together. I think even you can see the benefits in that.'

Alicia didn't trust his reasonable tone for a second. She felt sick but also, conversely, had to acknowledge her own silent misgivings about how young Melanie was and also Paolo's apparent youth and idealistic zeal. She had an uncanny feeling that both she and Dante were guilty of having sheltered their siblings from the harsher truths of the world. And in truth she was somewhat surprised at his own prescience in this regard.

She thought of something then. 'Why, when you knew it was Melanie, did you never mention Paolo? You *knew* that they'd been seeing each other.'

He stood again and paced back and forth with taut energy. He stopped and looked at her, hands on his hips. 'Because when you arrived, screaming all sorts of accusations about my involvement, I realised that Melanie was trying to set *me* up. You didn't mention Paolo once. It's obvious that she'd figured she'd get more out of me, and that you had gone along with her…but then Paolo arrived like an eager puppy, only too ready to accept responsibility.'

Alicia's lips were bloodless. 'That would be because she *told* him about the pregnancy and he came to be with her.' She shook her head. 'It's frightening how cynical you are.'

'Not cynical. Realistic, Alicia. That's why I came. I had to see for myself, make sure neither of you were planning on some big kind of tabloid kiss and tell.' His mouth twisted. 'That photo and the speculation about us is just about salvageable. As you can appreciate, with the delicacy of the merger, it would have a very adverse effect for the media to be focused on me in any kind of negative way and they are going to be watching our every move. Now that Paolo is here I'm prepared to allow—*for now*—that it was a misunderstanding.'

'That's big of you.'

She looked up at him then with defiance and yet a curious look of resignation. The image that came into Dante's head was of her asleep with her fists balled, ready to fight.

'What if I don't go back to Italy with you?'

'Do you really want to risk that? Paolo is under the impression that he is the one driving this great plan. But it's my house that they will be using, and ultimately my money that will be paying for Melanie's treatment and recuperation—something Paolo seems to be quite happy to ignore. Needless to say, at any moment, that could all be gone.'

'And you would really do that? Just to get back at me, at Melanie?'

A muscle twitched in his jaw. 'It doesn't have to descend to that, Alicia. I'm offering your sister everything on a plate, including the chance to be with Paolo and act her heart out. You just have to come with me today and be my hostess...'

And lover too...

Dante couldn't stop the word reverberating in his head. He knew without a doubt that there was no way he'd be able to keep his hands off her if she came with him today and, even if she wasn't acknowledging it yet to herself, she'd soon be made aware of it—this desire that even now pulsated through the air between them.

Alicia's mouth was grim, her face starkly pale. 'And with me close by your side, you'll be able to monitor my sister, make sure she isn't stealing the family silver.'

He smiled then and it wasn't friendly as he thought, *Exactly—you and your scheming sister won't make a move I'm not aware of...*

'*Cara*, my family didn't have any silver to steal, anything that's there has been hard won and paid for.'

His comment made Alicia's churning thoughts stop. What did he mean? And then she shook her head. She didn't care what he meant.

He was pulling his jacket from the couch and slipping it on with lithe grace. He walked to the door in a couple of long strides. 'I have some business to attend to in my office in London. I'll be back this evening, early. And I plan to leave tonight for Milan, returning to Lake Como tomorrow. If you decide you are going to come with me, have your bags packed and ready.' He looked at her clothes again. 'Actually, you don't need to pack, just bring yourself. We'll have to get you a decent wardrobe.'

Alicia opened her mouth in affront but, before she could say a word, he was continuing.

'I'll be outside here at seven p.m., I won't bother knocking. I'll wait for five minutes. That's it. It's up to you if you want to risk saying no.'

And, without a backward glance, he opened the door, shut it behind him and he was gone.

CHAPTER SIX

THAT EVENING ALICIA stood with a small holdall in one hand, the other on the lock of her front door. She could hear the idling purring engine of the car outside. It had, exactly as Dante had said, pulled up at precisely seven p.m. He irritated her with his attention to detail, his punctuality, his coolness. His *expectation*. The clock was ticking; she could hear it on the mantel.

Desperation clawed at her insides. She wanted to turn back the clock, drop her bag, dive under the covers of her bed and shut the world out. Shut Dante D'Aquanni out. But earlier that day she'd gone into the hospital and seeing Melanie and Paolo so happy, so delighted, so *together,* full of plans for moving into town…her escape route had been cut off, her fate decided. For the first time in her life, Melanie didn't *need* her and that isolated, rudderless feeling had swamped her again.

This was it. Her impulsive, over-protective actions had created this scenario. She really could not risk Melanie being subjected to Dante's censure or cynical disbelief. So she took a deep breath, turned the catch and pulled open the door. The sleek, dark car's engine revved for a second and Alicia panicked—was she too late? But then the revs fell again. A door was pushed open from the inside. The driver stepped out and Alicia could make out the outline of a dark shape in the back. She shivered and moved forward.

Dante had had to restrain himself from springing from the car. Five minutes had passed. He'd been sure she wasn't coming. Incensed beyond belief that a woman could be making him feel as if he were dangling on a string, he'd tersely instructed the driver to go. *But.* Then the door had opened and a feeling had flooded his entire body. A feeling he didn't want to acknowlege. When Alicia slipped into the seat beside him, she looked like a pale wraith. A waif. Still the shapeless clothes, still the pulled back hair. Irritation prickled across his skin.

'You've made the right decision.'

'As if I had a choice.' The door closed behind her shutting them into the confined intimate space. Darkness. Dante forced himself to relax. Taking his eyes away from her with more of an effort than he liked to admit, he looked out of the window as the car moved out of the estate and into the traffic.

'So how is this going to work, exactly?'

As his plane cruised above the English countryside, leaving it behind, Dante looked across at Alicia.

'We will stay in Milan tonight. I've booked you an appointment at a boutique there in the morning; we don't have much time to get you fitted and dressed. And made over. The guests arrive at the villa in three days.'

Alicia's spine straightened, her pride back with a vengeance. 'As you are aware I can't afford to buy myself an entire wardrobe. I must insist that you at least buy off-the-peg clothes. It would take me years to repay you for the designer wardrobe you seem to be insisting on.'

She looked unbelievably proud, like a tiny regal princess. Dante felt something move in his chest. He thrust it back down—back into the seething mass of twisted feelings and desire this woman aroused.

'Don't worry about the cost.'

'But I do, I will; it's an unnecessary expense.'

'It's not.' His eyes moved over her body with heated appraisal; she could feel her insides grow warm.

'As my partner, you will be expected to maintain a certain standard.'

Alicia wrestled with the poisonous memory of that brunette on the steps of the hotel—she was a *woman* in every sense of the word. And, as she processed what he was saying, she couldn't stop a look of disgust flashing across her face. She could just imagine the designer get-ups he'd expect to see her in. Dante saw her expression and it surprised him. He'd never had to justify wanting to buy a woman clothes before.

'A friend of mine is going to look after you.'

Alicia snorted. *A friend.* No doubt a previous lover who was bohemian enough to dress his current women. And it galled her that he'd been certain enough of her compliance that he'd already made the appointment. Her tardiness on leaving her apartment seemed childishly pathetic now.

His voice cut through her thoughts. 'She's eighty years old and has the mind of a steel trap. You can take that disparaging look off your face. Your opinion of my reputation is quite obvious and I won't have you making faces every time someone mentions a woman in connection with me.'

'And yet it's OK for everyone to think that I'm merely your new bit of fluff?'

'After the stunt you pulled, I think it's only fair. And necessary, as I've pointed out to you.'

Damn, did she have to be so argumentative? Already he was tempted to shut her up in a very satisfying way.

She turned more fully in her seat. She wasn't going to make

the mistake of standing up in the cabin again. 'Might I remind you that you were the one who initiated that kiss, not me.'

Dante felt an instinctive need to protect himself. His face was stiff, his hands were clenched. 'Should I have let you shout out to the world that I was the neglectful absentee father of your sister's baby? Your sister, who lay in a hospital in England in a grave condition? When I wasn't even aware of that fact?'

He shook his head, his eyes sparking. 'Luckily, I remembered your little outburst from the week before, so I had a fair idea of what you were going to say. I had to shut you up, that was all.'

Alicia sat back, deflated. He *hadn't* known of Melanie's accident. She would have been taking an unfair advantage. It killed her to admit that he did, in a way, have the moral high ground in this. And it also killed her somewhere to know that he'd kissed her with pure premeditated efficiency. And even though he'd kissed her yesterday too… She could recall his cool regard straight afterwards, as if he'd been conducting an experiment, as if his whole world hadn't gone up in flames, like hers had.

Waking up from a deep sleep, Alicia felt terror flood her bones. She was being held tight against a powerful body. It was dark; she didn't know where she was. She started to struggle fiercely, her mind clouding over in panic.

'Let me go, put me down.' The words wouldn't come out strong enough.

'*Dio!* You're like a cat; will you calm down? I'm only carrying you because even the plane landing didn't wake you up.'

Alicia tensed and stopped struggling immediately. Clarity rushed in. She was in Dante's arms. He was striding across the tarmac of the small private Milan airport. She wasn't working in the aid group any more. And then something she hadn't felt in such a long time—*if ever*—rushed through her.

She felt safe.

She looked up and saw a firm jaw clenched tightly. An implacable expression on his handsome face. She fought against relaxing against him and kept herself rigid until they reached a nearby car and he put her down. She couldn't look at him and just mumbled, 'I was having a dream…didn't know where I was.'

'Well, we're in Milan. Welcome back to Italy.'

He smiled grimly and Alicia looked at him then. The bottom fell out of her stomach. How bizarre to think she was safe when she knew she'd probably never been in more danger in her life.

He ushered her into the car and within half an hour they were pulling up outside a beautiful crumbling building. Still slightly disorientated from her heavy sleep—the relief of knowing that Melanie was on the mend and being minded meant she could finally relax—she moved as if blindfolded. She let Dante show her into a small, ancient yet luxuriously furnished palazzo, up to a bedroom where she closed the door behind her after a brief sterile goodnight.

She undressed in the dark, crawled under the covers and gave in to the much needed restorative sleep that claimed her again. Tomorrow…was her last thought. Tomorrow I'll think about what it meant to feel so safe, with him of all people…

When Alicia woke in the morning, it was to a gentle knocking and her door being opened by a shy pretty girl in jeans and a casual top.

'*Buon giorno…*'

'*Boun giorno,*' Alicia repeated sleepily, a little bemused as the girl came in and pulled back heavy curtains.

She turned and smiled at Alicia. She spoke in halting English, clearly having rehearsed her speech. 'Signore D'Aquanni said to wake you and tell you that he is in the dining room having breakfast.'

Alicia smiled weakly as orientation rushed back, 'Thank you… *Grazie.*'

The girl left and closed the door quietly after her. Alicia flopped back on to the huge pillow. She couldn't remember the last time she'd woken to feel so clear, restored, refreshed. And so confused and bewildered at the remarkable chain of events.

The memory of waking last night to find herself being carried in Dante's arms flashed back into her head. She tensed. She knew that she was being a coward, but in an effort to avoid thinking about how that had made her feel, she perversely opted for going directly into the lion's den.

A short time later she found her way downstairs and into a charming, bright dining room. A big polished table with a stunning vase of extravagant blooms at one end of the polished mahogany. And Dante D'Aquanni at the other end, sipping coffee and reading a paper. He looked up and his eyes seemed to bore right through her.

'Sleep well?'

The tension that seemed ever present around them hummed like an electrical charge. She nodded. 'Like a baby.'

She walked over and sat down and the same young girl came in with orange juice, fresh coffee, croissants, fruit. Alicia hadn't seen such a feast in so long that her stomach rumbled loudly. With her face going pink, she looked over and saw Dante smiling at the young girl as she poured him more coffee. It made the room tilt dizzily. That smile should come with a health warning, she thought, even as she itched to wipe it from his face.

'Alicia, this is Patrizia, the daughter of my housekeeper, Rosa. She's working here for her summer holidays and giving her *mamma* a break.'

Alicia was glad of the distraction, her face was still burning. She looked up. 'Hello, Patrizia.'

The girl blushed, giggled lightly and left the room.

Alicia sighed. A serious case of hero worship. And who could blame the girl? She busied herself with food, feeling her appetite return for the first time in days. That made her think of the pasta

Dante had had sent up to her in her room in the villa at Lake Como. The way the housekeeper had taken care of her. The way he'd just smiled at Patrizia. She sneaked a glance at him. He was engrossed in the paper, long brown fingers holding it up. And then she remembered the feeling of his hand on her breast, the calluses. The evidence that his hands weren't soft, but *hard*. Her breathing stopped, her nipples tightened. She dropped her knife with a jarring clatter and Dante looked up with a frown.

'Sorry...' Alicia furiously willed down the rising tide of shame.

He put down the paper and Alicia concentrated on spreading jam on a rapidly crumbling croissant.

'I've booked you into the boutique this morning, we leave in an hour.'

She looked up, her hands stilling. *'We?'*

He nodded. 'I have some things to attend to at my offices here; I'll drop you off and come back to pick you up.'

'Oh.' Relief flooded her.

He smiled and it was predatory. 'Shopping has always bored me to tears, so don't worry, not even the thought of seeing your delectable form draped in all kinds of silk would induce me to sit for hours while you posture and preen.'

And simultaneously, as he said those words, Dante had a sudden fantasy image of her naked body, wrapped only in silk, and couldn't imagine anything he'd want to see more. Before he could give himself away—his out of control reactions—he drained his coffee and stood. 'I'll see you in the hall, then.'

Alicia's mouth gaped as she watched him leave, a whole list of retorts which she hadn't had the chance to get out trembling on her lips. *Posture and preen?* She hadn't postured and preened even in her teenage make-up experimentation years. The man was insufferable. And, even more disconcerting, he thought her form *delectable?* She took a big gulp of coffee and yelped in pain when it burned her mouth.

CHAPTER SEVEN

'I'LL be back for you in a couple of hours. I'm looking forward to never seeing those shapeless garments again.'

Alicia had her hand on the car door handle and nearly fell out when the driver opened it for her. She just looked at Dante murderously. Her mouth still smarted painfully from the coffee. She wanted to say something—anything—and had to settle for an incoherent grunt.

'Ciao…' came softly from behind her in the car and she took great pleasure in slamming the door shut, much to the driver's surprise.

Two hours passed quickly. Alicia hadn't known that it was possible to spend so much time in one shop. Between fittings, she'd stood in her tatty underwear, surrounded by fabric and shoes. It was the kind of place where you had to ring a bell to get in and when she'd arrived she'd almost expected to be turned away, and had wondered for a second what she would do if that happened. Alone with no money in a foreign city. No phone number for Dante, no phone. Instead of feeling relief, she'd actually felt something much more confusing.

But then the door had opened and a tall woman with silver-grey hair and impeccable carriage had taken one look at her and said in perfect English, 'Ah. You must be Alicia. Dante described you perfectly. I am Signora Pasquale.'

Alicia's cheeks had burned for about the umpteenth time that morning, as the woman and her assistants had proceeded to strip her completely. Every now and then the very intimidating Signora would come in and look at Alicia, tutting, 'You are *so* tiny. What can I do?' And, with her arms in the air, she'd go off again.

Eventually Alicia heard the bell ring authoritatively and *knew* it was him. Stupidly, she wrapped her arms around herself, even though she knew he wouldn't see her. Butterflies fluttered in her belly. She heard the low rumble of his voice, the tinkling laughter of Signora Pasquale and, even though the woman was eighty, something very disturbing flared in Alicia's chest. One of the assistants came in then with rosy cheeks. Alicia's mouth tightened. She was going to start calling it the Dante effect.

'Here are some casual clothes; the Signora had them delivered. They will do you for day wear until the main clothes arrive at Signore D'Aquanni's villa in a couple of days.'

The girl held out a beautifully folded pile of clothes and what looked like a leather weekend bag, also full of clothes. When Alicia unfolded them she found a silk camisole top in burnished copper, a cream skirt and matching underwear. Kitten heel sandals in a dark complementary gold—very simple, very Italian and very stylish. As much as she hated this—the waste and extravagance—the feel of the silky fabric against her skin made her close her eyes with a stirring of guilty pleasure. It had been so long since she'd let herself feel anything like it.

With the bag in one hand and the matching jacket of the suit in the other, Alicia emerged. Dante was sitting down, drinking a cup of coffee, talking to the designer. He looked up and his hand stilled on the way to his mouth. His whole body stilled. Apart from the tantalizing glimpses he'd had while she'd lain sleeping on the bed in his villa and that all too brief moment in his lap on the plane, he'd had to imagine her shape.

She looked at him defiantly and Dante felt as if they were the only two people in the room, the designer and her assistants forgotten. What she was wearing wasn't in any way overtly sexy but…with her delicate curves filling it out, he'd never seen anyone so alluring. Everything was in proportion—every curve, every swell. He imagined spanning her waist with one hand. Her skin was lightly tanned—soft and silky. For the first time in his life, he was rendered speechless.

Alicia tilted her chin. If he didn't stop staring at her as if she were some kind of alien just landed on planet earth she was going to scream. Thankfully, Signora Pasquale got up and fussed around her. 'Oh, good. These clothes fit perfectly. They will see you through the next few days and we will have the rest delivered by your plane as soon as they are ready.' She looked at Dante. 'This time of the month I presume it'll be on its usual run?'

Dante nodded absently. Alicia blanched and looked at the woman. *By plane?* Dante saw her reaction and stood smoothly, coming over and taking Alicia's bag, guiding her out of the shop with a hand on her upper arm, burning it.

In the car she rounded on him. 'Is a plane really necessary just to bring clothes for me to wear? I mean, really, that is the absolute height of—'

'Alicia—' his voice was like the crack of a whip '—I can afford it and—'

'I don't—' she tried to interject, but he raised a hand, stopping her.

'If this is just a facade, a veneer of trendy environmental concern, then give it up now, because I'm not interested. You might try to pretend to others that you didn't leave your bleeding heart behind in Africa, but you won't fool me.'

Alicia gasped. 'It's not a veneer or a facade. If you can justify sending an entire airplane into the skies just to bring me some clothes, then go right ahead. And if you can sleep with your conscience, then so be it, but I think it's *disgusting.*'

Dante watched her with fascination. She was leaning forward, face alive, luminous. And all he wanted to sleep with right then was *her.* Her quick condemnation burned him again but he would not give in to the satisfaction of telling her the truth. Let her stew.

'Well, then, you'd better get ready to be disgusted because we're on the way to take a helicopter to Lake Como right now. And just remember, you weren't disgusted when that plane was available to take you back to England at a moment's notice.'

She couldn't tear her eyes away from the censure in his. Yet again he'd managed to make her feel in the wrong.

She turned her head and looked unseeingly out of the window, her whole body tense and taut. She felt unbelievably exposed in the silky top and flimsy skirt. The silk of the new panties was also an unwelcome sensual reminder every time she moved, of the man who lounged on the seat only inches away. Little had she known that her actions would have brought her to this…back in Italy, to be paraded as Dante D'Aquanni's newest lover. She might as well be part of the harem of some desert king. What she'd just endured was the equivalent of being washed and sent to his tent.

Dante ached with the restraint it took not to reach out and haul her into his lap. But he imposed an iron will and he'd just remembered something. Her apparent ease and knowledge of the helicopter must have come from working with them in Africa. It made something uncomfortable lodge in his chest, and for the rest of the journey they were mutually silent.

The same benignly smiling housekeeper showed Alicia to her room. It was a different one from the one she'd spent that night in. The room she'd been *locked* in. She tried to hang on to that feeling of outrage as she sat on the bed and looked around, but it was hard. It was fading. Dante had surprised her by showing her where the study was and informing her that she could use it whenever she wanted to call Melanie.

Then he'd handed her over to the housekeeper, who he'd introduced as Julieta, and informed her that they'd eat at five p.m. He'd told her to make herself at home. A far cry from the last time. She stood somewhat shakily and went to look out of the window. The lake was spread out before her and took her breath away in the early afternoon sunshine.

Exploring a little, she looked around the room, found the *en suite* bathroom and then another door. Assuming it to be a dressing room, she opened it, only to find herself in another bedroom. *His.* She knew it without a doubt. It was huge, dominated by a massive king-size bed. Simple yet discreetly elegant furnishings—not too stark and masculine but enough of a stamp to make it unmistakably male.

At that moment his door opened and Alicia stood there, her eyes growing round, transfixed when he walked in. He was pulling off his tie, undoing the top button of his shirt and then stopped, seeing her.

His eyes raked her up and down. Took in her slight form, the jacket gone, the smooth skin of her shoulders bared. Took in her exquisitely shaped calves, her tiny bare feet. She had kicked off her shoes. Her hair was pulled back and one long tendril lay over her shoulder.

'I thought this might be a dressing room…'

Dante spread out an arm, a hard smile playing around that seductive mouth. 'By all means, you can dress in here if you want.'

She stood stiffly. 'You know what I mean.' She turned. 'I'll go. Sorry for disturbing you.'

He muttered something in Italian behind her and she turned again. 'Excuse me?'

He looked slightly tortured for a second and something in that look made an answering quiver erupt deep in her groin. But she couldn't trust what she'd seen—it had to be her mind playing tricks.

'Nothing. Go. You should rest. You're going to need it.'

A fear of something powerful moving through her made her blurt out, 'Do we have to have adjoining rooms?'

He nodded and walked towards her. She backed away. 'The guests will expect that we will be sharing a room, not merely occupying adjoining rooms, but here we can get away with it.'

She shook her head. 'But—'

He interrupted her. 'But when we go to South Africa we *will* share a room, whether you like it or not.'

Alicia's head swirled ominously. 'Hang on a second.' She put out a hand. as if that might stop him from advancing. 'South Africa? Since when were we going to South Africa?' She felt all the conflicting emotions arise again—the reason she'd run there in the first place, the heartache, the unimaginable pain she'd witnessed, the physical pain, hardship and *scars* she still bore.

Dante saw the colour drain from her face and frowned. 'I said that the *first* week would be here. South Africa is the venue for the last two weeks and the main part of the negotiations. That's where we're proposing to finalize the deal and embark on our first project which will be the construction of a huge sports stadium just outside Cape Town. That has been at the centre of this merger. Thousands of companies competed for the job and we got it on the basis of the merger being successful. So even *that* at this stage hangs in the balance.'

Alicia felt weak. She wanted to sit down. 'You never mentioned that.'

'What's wrong?' he asked sharply, coming closer.

Alicia stepped back jerkily. She felt far too vulnerable to be under close scrutiny.

'Nothing.' She tried to smile, 'I just hadn't expected to be going back there so soon, that's all…' She'd be fine. She wasn't going back to the same place. She'd be at the other end of the continent. She turned and put one foot in front of the other. 'I'll see you at five.'

And once in her own room, she closed the door and leant back against it breathing shallow breaths. She'd had no idea the thought of returning to Africa would affect her this badly.

Minutes later she paced up and down the floor. It wasn't as if she'd experienced any more or any less than any of the other aid workers. But still…the remembered fear gripped her and the pain seemed to flare in her lower back…it could have been so much worse. And she'd stuck it out after that, determined not to be weak, to give in…but then when *he'd* arrived, that had been the final straw and she'd returned home. And that still made her feel guilty. That she'd let a man influence her actions—*again*. He'd driven her there, and then away too…

She sat down on the bed and felt cold. She didn't want to think about him, but right now there were too many uncanny similarities.

Raul Carro. Dr Raul Carro. The man who had taken her heart and watched it beating in his hands before calmly crushing it to pieces.

Or at least that was what it had felt like at the time. Almost two years ago now. The dark and dashing Spanish doctor working briefly in England had captivated her, and her heart.

And here she was, in close proximity to another of his ilk. Too good looking and powerful for his own good. A Latin magician. She knew this situation was nothing like the one with Raul, who had seduced her with ruthless guile. And she was quite certain that the physical contact Dante had initiated so far was nothing but cold calculation, designed to unnerve her. So why did she feel then as though she were on a precipice, about to fall off again?

It was only when in her shower a short time later that shock stilled Alicia's body as she remembered Dante's assertion that they would be sharing a room in South Africa. She rested her forehead against the tiled wall under the spray. Dark and treacherous desire rose up to taunt her. And then she stood straight. She would not allow herself to be used like that again. She *would* protect herself this time. And she got on with scrubbing her body. It wasn't as if Dante D'Aquanni was really attracted to her anyway. A man like him would play around with her for pure idle sport.

CHAPTER EIGHT

THAT EVENING AT dinner Alicia tried to eat her wild mushroom soup, pulling again at the top which kept slipping down her shoulder. She had changed purely because the skirt and camisole top had felt too flimsy, too revealing, but this was almost worse.

Dante felt prickly and irritable. He'd spent the afternoon castigating himself for insisting on bringing this woman here. And all the very good, *valid* reasons for bringing her here had immediately jumped out at him, not least of which was the fact that he still didn't trust her or her sister an inch. But he knew, if he was honest with himself, that all of his reasons were about as rock-solid as he'd wish to make them. If he didn't desire her as much as he did, and if that top fell off her shoulder one more time—he stopped his fevered thoughts—then he knew she wouldn't be here, it was as simple as that.

Alicia put down her spoon and yanked the top up again, but already the material was making its treacherous descent. She sighed and gave up. She heard an inarticulate sound and looked up to see Dante staring at her with such intensity that her insides melted.

'What…what is it?'

'Leave your top alone,' he gritted out.

Alicia felt confused for a second. 'My…oh…'

And as if on cue, the shoulder of the light golden silk top slipped again, baring her down to her upper arm. Alicia had hummed and hawed before picking it out of the bag earlier. It had been the next most casual thing in there, along with the linen trousers. She wasn't able to wear a bra as its design was meant to show off the shoulders.

His voice sounded tortured. 'It's meant to fall like that.'

Dio! Didn't she know that?

Alicia's stomach felt tight. 'I know that. I'm just trying not to look like some half naked wanton as we eat dinner. I'd be much happier in my own clothes—'

Dante shuddered delicately. 'No. They should be burned.'

Alicia rolled her eyes. 'I mean my real own clothes. My suitcase didn't make the journey home. *That's* why I had a limited wardrobe to choose from. I did a big clear out before going to Africa and, as Melanie is about five inches taller than me, her clothes swamp me. It might be hard to believe, but I'm not a total hick, Dante.'

The hand which held his spoon fell back to the plate and he frowned lightly.

All of a sudden, all she could see and think about was how handsome and compelling Dante looked dressed, in a black shirt and dark trousers. She chattered to fill the silence. 'I mean, you must wear jeans sometimes. T-shirts?'

'That's the first time you've said my name.'

'Didn't your—*what?*'

'The first time you've said my name.'

So she had. And it had come out easily—too easily—without thinking. Familiarly. Alicia shrugged and the feel of a light breeze on her bare skin made her shiver slightly. She focused on her soup. 'Well, I'm going to have to get used to it. I presume I can't be calling you Mr D'Aquanni in front of the others…'

Dante studied her downbent head, the silken mass of corkscrew curls pulled back and up in a haphazard knot, showing the clean, elegant lines of her neck. When she'd said his name it had reached out and curled itself around his senses, pulling on them with sensual promise.

'No,' he said and his voice was curt. His eyes rested on the tempting, smooth curve of that bare shoulder and he shifted in his seat. A heavy tension seemed to envelop them as neither spoke, and it was only when Julieta came in with the next course that Alicia felt she could breathe again.

'Come out to the terrace; Julieta will serve us coffee there.'

It didn't sound as if she had a choice. Alicia stood and preceded Dante out of the dining room. Again, she had that sensation of déjà vu. Only a couple of days ago she had fainted at the man's feet in this very hall and now she was dressed in silk and linen, walking out to the terrace to take some after dinner coffee. She was very aware of him behind her. Her skin prickled and she felt goosebumps come up.

The air outside was warm and silky. Still. It was so quiet and the lake looked so beautiful in the lingering dusk that it took Alicia's attention away from her situation for a second. She went and rested her hands on the wall, breathing in the scent of fragrant flowers, and felt some kind of weight lift from her shoulders, which was a bizarre sensation to admit to, here, with him.

'It's beautiful, isn't it?'

She looked up at the man beside her. His face was transfixed, totally relaxed. Her breath was taken all over again, as much with her rogue imagination as anything else. 'Yes.' And she knew she wasn't talking about the lake.

He looked down at her and she coloured, mortified to be caught staring. A mocking glint in his dark eyes drove her away from the wall and she chose a single seat behind them. She was burningly aware of the way the fabric of the top felt against her bare breasts. It felt…bold, but also sensuous, like going skinny-dipping. Dante kept looking at her, she could feel it as she reso-lutely looked the other way and crossed her arms over her chest to disguise the betraying steepling of her nipples.

Julieta appeared with coffee and Alicia helped her with the tray, relaxing for a moment in the other woman's easy presence. When she handed Dante his cup, he came and took it with a funny look on his face.

Alicia quickly took a big gulp from her own cup and winced, gasping in pain as the hot liquid burnt her still sensitive mouth from where she'd burned it only that morning. She put down the cup with a clatter. Dante was beside her instantly.

'What is it?'

Alicia shook her head, her eyes smarting. 'I burnt my mouth this morning and just got it again…I'm fine, really.'

Dante was hunched down beside her, looking up, a hand on her knee. The pain faded in Alicia's mouth as all she could seem to feel was her heart thumping heavily, loudly, in the silence. He was looking up at her with a dangerous glint in his eyes, his hand heavy on her leg, burning through her clothes. Alicia's heart clenched. *Oh, no, please…*

Dante stood with lithe grace and pulled her up with him. Their bodies were very close. Both his hands went around the back of her head, her jaw. She couldn't breathe. Her hands were clenched by her sides. Arms rigid.

'What…what are you doing? I'm fine.'

He shook his head softly, the burning light in his eyes drowning out any coherent thought in Alicia's head. 'Just checking… Open your mouth.'

Stupidly, Alicia did. She felt foggy, heavy…

'Show me your tongue.'

Stupidly, she did that too.

It was the sight of that small pink tongue that drove him over the edge. His thumb snagged her lower lip, her tongue darted back in and a flush stained her cheeks. He could feel her breathing change, grow more rapid. The pulse in her neck beat frantically against his wrist.

'Dante…really, I'm a nurse. It's nothing.'

'*This*…is not nothing.'

Alicia knew he wasn't talking about her mouth being burnt. She was valiantly clinging on to the hope and belief that he was, though, clinging on to it right up until his head descended and his mouth settled over hers.

At the moment their mouths touched Alicia felt a sigh move through her—a sigh of inevitability. And a fierce exultant force that terrified her. So here was the evidence—he did find her attractive. One arm was wrapped around her back pulling her into him and the other hand threaded through her hair to cup the back of her head, tilting and angling her so that he could plunder her mouth. And that was what it felt like. She was being *plundered* right to the tips of her toes.

Her hands had to hold on to something and she found herself clasping his waist, the trim lean lines. His belly was hard and taut against her breasts which seemed to swell in direct response. It was as if she were literally flowering beneath this man's touch. His tongue touched hers, stroked and danced. Drawing back, he nipped gently on her lower lip before returning and making her feel so boneless with mounting need that she couldn't stop herself trembling uncontrollably.

He drew back and looked down. She found it hard to look up, her head heavy. It was as if she were drugged, incapable of moving, thinking, could hardly open her eyes.

Then a gust of slightly cooler evening air danced between them and it was as if a bucket of cold water had been thrown in her face. She stiffened and pulled out of his arms and, taken aback with the suddenness of her movement, he let her go. It was all very clear to Alicia right now. What she needed to remember, what she'd forgotten in a shockingly short amount of time.

She looked up to Dante's face and willed herself to stand tall, strong, when everything in her wanted to hurl herself back into his arms and beg him to kiss her again.

'I don't know what just happened there—'

He advanced with a dangerous look on his face. 'I can show you if you like.' He clearly didn't like the direction things were going. Alicia retreated around the back of the seat and gripped it. Her top slid off her shoulder again.

'That won't be happening again. Just because you have me here as a result of extenuating circumstances, just because you've dressed me, does not mean that I am available sexually. I am not interested, do you hear me? I will not be used like this just because it's…it's easy or convenient.'

Dante regarded the woman in front of him. Two spots of high colour marked her cheeks, her mouth looked like a ripe, moist fruit… Her hair was coming undone, tendrils of curls falling in sexy disarray. He felt anything but easy or convenient right now. He felt hot and wanted very much to take her back into his arms and slake that sizzling in his veins. *Dio.* When he thought about that night with Alessandra Macchi, the desire he had felt for her wouldn't even register a blip on this radar.

He had no doubt in his mind that he would indeed be taking Alicia Parker to bed. She was here now, his for a month. Plenty of time. She wouldn't last more than a week with this heat burning up the air around them.

So he ignored the rampant pulse in his trousers and smiled urbanely. 'Please forgive me. Of course I wouldn't want you to feel anything but a happy guest while you're here.'

Alicia looked at him suspiciously. *A happy guest?* Hardly. More like an executive prisoner. He was up to something. The silk of the top chafed against tight nipples and she fought against looking down to see if they were as prominent as they felt. She had to get out of there. Now.

'If that's all, it's been a long day; I'm going to go to bed.'

Dante nodded and gestured with an arm. Bidding her goodnight, he watched her walk away. His face changed in an instant into an expression so brooding and intense that if she had turned back and seen it she would have run for the hills.

CHAPTER NINE

FOR THE NEXT couple of days the villa was transformed from an oasis of calm to a hive of activity as caterers, more household staff, gardeners and security men all worked to get things ready for the arrival of the VIPs. Alicia wandered around, thankful that Dante seemed to be firmly ensconced in his office most of the time, no doubt preparing for the conference. Ducking out of the way of two men carrying in a huge display of exotically coloured blue flowers, she followed them curiously. She'd been too intimidated so far to explore too much but now she followed the men into a huge dining room. She gasped with pure delight. The walls were an exquisite shade of blue and the ceiling was made up of panels of reflective glass. It was so unusual, she'd never seen anything like it in her life. It was all at once decadent, *old* and inherently modern.

The men had stopped and were holding the display awkwardly near the huge table, which dominated the room. They looked at her expectantly and one of them said something.

Alicia looked back at them, had she missed something? 'Scusi...I don't speak Italian. Would you like to see the house-keeper?'

A dryly amused voice came from close behind her, making her jump.

'They think you're the mistress of the villa; they want to know where to put the flowers.'

Alicia's breath was momentarily driven from her lungs when she looked at Dante. It was the first time she'd seen him all day. And for the first time he was dressed down, in jeans and a shirt. Her pulse jumped to vibrant life. She swung her gaze back to the men and tried to smile, shaking her head. 'No...no.' Attempting to show in sign language that she and Dante weren't man and wife, she only ended up with two...three laughing men looking at her. Dante said a few rapid words and the delivery men left the flowers in the middle of the table and walked out shaking their heads, still laughing.

Alicia crossed her arms and tilted her head back, barriers springing up rapidly. 'Is it always this amusing making fun of foreigners?'

He surprised her by taking her hand and leading her into the room, and heat travelled up her arm. Alicia followed Dante with her heart in her mouth. His hand was huge and warm around hers. And his familiar action threatened to crumble those precious barriers. Her mind worked overtime; he must be using another tactic, getting her used to his touch so that when the others arrived—

'This room is the oldest in the villa.'

Alicia looked away from him reluctantly, seriously afraid that he was going to pounce. 'It is beautiful. I haven't been in here before.'

Dante gestured up to the ceiling. 'Those panels have been there since the mid sixteenth century—Venetian glass—and that blue on the walls is such an unusual colour because it too is from that time.'

'Wow...' Alicia breathed, her mind distracted but her body still very aware of her hand clasped in his. His hard palms surprised her again, made her think of how they had felt on her breast, how they might feel elsewhere. She forced her rampant imagination to cool down. 'You're very lucky to have grown up with such a wealth of culture.'

He dropped her hand abruptly and moved away, his head rearing back. Alicia felt bewildered—what had she said?

Dante's face was like granite. 'You keep alluding to my so-called *background;* you obviously didn't bother too hard to check the facts when you came looking for me.'

Alicia was seriously nonplussed now. She shook her head. 'I'm sorry; I don't know what you mean.'

Dante flicked a glance around the room and gave a short harsh laugh. 'This villa isn't *my* family home; I bought it just three years ago. All of my homes are recent acquisitions.' His mouth tightened as if he was trying to stop himself. He waged an inner battle that was only too apparent in the harsh glint of his eyes and a pulse beating in his temple as he said finally, 'I don't come from this, Alicia, much as it might be more palatable to you. I come from the streets of Naples, where you fight for a space, a corner. And that is your home. Was my home.'

'So please don't presume to know what I grew up with, because it was light years away from a place like this...'

Alicia wanted to bite her tongue, swallow back the words. She put out a hand instinctively but he just moved further away. 'I'm sorry, Dante; I had no idea.'

'No, because you're like everyone else—eager to capitalize on the wealth that is so conveniently available to you now. Who cares where it came from, *si?*'

She swallowed convulsively. 'That's not fair. I don't care how you made your money. I would never have come after you if I hadn't thought it was the only option.'

The injured look in her eyes was making him feel claustrophobic.

'Yes, well, you did and you're here now. I have some work to return to.'

He strode from the room and turned at the door, a very cynical twist to his mouth, 'By the way, your clothes will be here tomorrow morning and a driver will be outside in half an hour to take you into Bellagio; I've booked you into a local beauty salon for the afternoon.'

And, with those curtly delivered words, he was gone, leaving Alicia reeling. And, ridiculously, all she could think about was how insulting it was that he believed she needed an entire afternoon in a beauty salon.

Dante went straight outside and gulped in big lungfuls of air. Damn it. *What the hell had just happened there?* His hands were fisted on his hips, tension radiated in waves off his body, keeping the workers milling around him at a distance.

Why hadn't he just spilled his guts out entirely? Why stop at telling her the bare bones of the dismal truth of growing up on the streets?

Two days under his roof: he desired her and now he wanted to tell her about himself? Why had her assumption that he'd grown up with a silver spoon in his mouth made him lash out like that? He didn't care what people thought. Not any more. He was proud of his roots, made no real secret of it. If anything, he was feted for it by those who knew. Not always for the right reasons, though. He'd seen the way women looked at him— women from a certain social class, hungrily, with covetous lust, attracted to the untamed part of him... It turned his stomach.

And she...she was no better than any of them. She was the same. But she was more dangerous. Because, somehow, she was getting under his skin in a way that hadn't happened in a long time. So long, in fact, that he could remember exactly when. *That* had been the major lesson in his life. Not learning to survive among the gangs in Naples, not protecting his younger brother, not even becoming a billionaire with homes on practically every continent. He had learnt his most valuable lesson at the hands of a woman and he wasn't about to make the same mistake twice.

He turned back to the villa. He could handle this, could handle her. Was he really scared of being made a fool of by a tiny five foot nothing temptress? All she was good for was warming his bed and that, he vowed, was going to happen very soon.

Alicia returned from a surprisingly enjoyable afternoon spent in the salon. Contrary to what she had feared—some kind of reality TV make over experience where she'd emerge looking like a generic bimbo complete with boob job—it had consisted of nothing more sinister than a facial, massage, pedicure, manicure and a trim. The hair stylist had waxed lyrical about her hair colour—courtesy of the African sun—her natural curls, and had barely changed a thing.

Even though there were evidently far more staff in residence now, the villa seemed to have reverted momentarily to its hushed peace, the work having stopped for the evening. Julieta greeted Alicia at the door, another beaming smile in place as she handed her a note. She smiled her thanks and took it. Opening it, the large scrawl immediately brought a dark, handsome face to mind.

I've had to go into Milan to tie up some last-minute arrangements. I won't be back until shortly before the main welcome drinks tomorrow night. My assistant Alex will be arriving in the morning to oversee welcoming the guests. All you have to do is be ready for me at seven p.m., I'll meet you in your room. Please dress appropriately for dinner. Dante.

The short sharp sentences with the bare minimum of information brought Alicia back down to earth with a thud. She had

actually felt a weird and totally inappropriate sense of owner-
ship coming back to the villa, had had a fizz of anticipation in
her veins at the thought of seeing Dante again. Had even
wondered if he'd notice anything different about her...if he'd
like it.

She crumpled up the note and threw it in the bin in her room.
She took a long hard look at herself in the mirror. To entertain
any kind of softening towards Dante D'Aquanni was to invite
catastrophe. She knew that now. Especially after his incendiary
kisses. She couldn't afford to forget Raul Carro. But...the awful
thing was, Raul Carro was becoming harder and harder to visu-
alize, harder and harder to remember.

Her face tightened. She couldn't afford to forget that Dante
was the same animal, albeit in different clothes. A man like him
would only ever use her ruthlessly before discarding her. Wasn't
he already doing that?

Turning away from her image, her expressively wistful eyes
which told another story entirely, Alicia firmly pushed Dante
from her mind and went downstairs to call home. She had explained this whole situation in a very vague way to Melanie,
making it sound as if she was doing Dante a favour because he
needed a hostess...Melanie hadn't seen the tabloid spread or
thought to question her too much, thankfully.

After nearly an hour spent on the phone listening to her
sister's excited chatter about being discharged the next day,
Alicia hung up. While she hated the power that Dante wielded
in regard to her sister's well-being, right at that moment Alicia
could have wept with relief...

It was nearing seven the following evening and Alicia was
in a state of high nervous tension. She'd been acutely aware of
the time ticking by all day and just a short while before had heard
the sound of the helicopter returning. *Dante.* In fact, there'd been
nothing but the sound of arrivals all day, cars pulling up, the
sounds of staff running up and down stairs and corridors. Frantic

hushed tones. Alicia had kept well back, terrified in case anyone expected her to account for her presence there.

At nine o'clock that morning she'd opened her bedroom door to a man roughly about the same age as Dante D'Aquanni. He was blond, short and had mischievous blue eyes. He'd introduced himself as Alex, Dante's assistant, and had told Alicia that he would be handling the meeting and greeting of all the guests. She hadn't failed to notice the way his eyes had been very assessing, openly curious as to what on earth his boss might see in this woman.

Alicia had straightened her spine, feeling justifiably vulnerable. She had no idea what Dante may or may not have told his assistant and hated the feeling that perhaps he *knew*…but he had seemed nice enough and had checked in on her during the day to make sure she was being looked after. So she couldn't fault him really.

And now the clock's hands were nearly at seven p.m. But still she jumped when the knock came on their shared door. The walls were so thick that she hadn't heard a movement from his room. She took a deep breath and turned away from her reflection, knowing that she'd done all she could in terms of trying to make herself presentable.

'Come in.'

The butterflies turned into small birds beating against her chest. The door seemed to open in slow motion. He was just a dark shape at first, the light blocking him out so that for a second he could see her but she couldn't see him.

Dante pushed open the door and felt a curious trepidation in his chest. What *the hell was that?* But it wouldn't go away and, as he walked in, the evening sun moved at that split second and Alicia stood there, bathed in a halo of light. Banal words like stunning, gorgeous, came into his head, but really didn't do her justice. She wore a deep, deep red dress. It was silk, it was strapless, it fell to her knees and had a slit up the side. It clung to soft, feminine curves. It was simple, artful and provocative enough to make him want to stride over, strip it off and lay her down on the nearby bed. His hand gripped the doorknob.

The sun shifted again, the light fading and Dante's mouth quirked. He was seeing things, that was all. Alicia Parker scrubbed up well. That was it. He strode forward, his feelings and turbulent desires firmly under control.

Alicia felt unbelievably nervous as he came in. He'd stood there for a long moment and she hadn't been able to see the expression on his face with the setting sun in her eyes. But now he was here, the quintessential billionaire in his tuxedo, white shirt and black bow-tie. Her breath stalled and she said very jerkily, 'I hope this is OK; I wasn't sure what to put on.'

Why did she have to look so damn nervous? It made all sorts of conflicting things rise up again, that control laughably crumbling.

'It's fine.' He was terse. 'What have you done to your hair?'

She put a hand up, her face flushing. 'Should I take it down? I was trying something the hairdresser showed me yesterday.'

'No, it's fine.' Dante's voice was gruff. Her hair was magnificent. Caught back and tied in a careless bun to the side, it looked sexy and chic. He put a hand on her bare shoulder, turning her around, and her skin felt soft and warm. A red diamanté hair-clip sparkled amongst the dark golden strands.

'It's fine,' he repeated. 'Let's go or we'll be late.'

Alicia grabbed a shawl and followed him somewhat unsteadily, unaccustomed to the high heels. At the top of the stairs he waited for her, a look of impatience on his face. Her heart sank; he still hadn't forgiven her for her innocent assumptions. And then, as if she'd imagined it, the look disappeared and something else was there. Something…*hot* and unfathomable. When she reached him, he took her hand and lifted it to his mouth, pressing a kiss to the underside of her wrist. It felt like a shockingly intimate gesture and colour scorched her cheeks.

'Ah, D'Aquanni, there you are!' a voice boomed out from the bottom of the stairs and Alicia realized that they were in full view of the open door leading into the main drawing room, which in turn led into the dining room. Dante's grip on her hand tightened. He was putting on an act, making it look genuine. That was all. Alicia felt like a prize fool. She'd actually thought for a split second... Her eyes flashed and she sent a very pointed look back at him, tightening her own fingers around his as if to say, *I know it's an act too...* She smiled up at him and it was hard and brittle.

And she didn't have time to know if she'd fooled him or not as he led her down the stairs to meet the owner of the booming voice.

CHAPTER TEN

ALICIA sipped from her glass of vintage champagne and tried not to let a bemused smile show on her face. The scene around her was so far removed from where she'd spent the last year—or anywhere, if she was honest—that it was almost funny. But then she looked at Dante's impressive back and any thoughts of smiling fled as heat unfurled in her belly.

Dante had been sucked into a round of greetings and Alicia was hanging back feeling shy, a little bewildered at the sight of new people, all bedecked in their finery. Apart from Buchanen and O'Brien, there were about five men and two women, the various assistants and advisers attached to each man. They all looked fearsomely important and the room reeked of wealth—the kind of wealth that would make your head spin.

The man at the bottom of the stairs had been Derek O'Brien, Dante's fellow construction entrepreneur from Dublin and obviously his close friend. Derek had said he was accompanied by his wife, one of the few, it seemed, who was allowed the honour of attending this week. Just as Alicia was wondering about this, a nice-looking woman approached her.

'Hello, you must be Alicia.'

Alicia nodded and shook the woman's hand, smiling shyly. 'Yes…I'm sorry and you are?'

'I'm Patricia O'Brien, Derek's wife. I believe you just met. He told me to come and make sure you were all right.'

Alicia felt a dart of something as she realized that Dante obviously hadn't been concerned about her. They'd walked in and he'd been surrounded in seconds by a crush of people, barely looking back to see if she was still there.

Alicia was glad of the friendly greeting. 'You're very good.'

'I see that even though she was invited too, Buchanen's wife hasn't come for the first week; probably knew she'd be sidelined…' The older woman shook her head wryly. 'My husband, however, is incapable of doing anything without me.'

Patricia was looking fondly at her husband across the room and Alicia felt envious. She took a hurried sip of the sparkling wine. What was wrong with her? She'd never felt that lack before.

She felt a prickling on the back of her neck and looked up. Dante was reaching out a hand through the throng and, like the Red Sea parting, people stood back and let her through. She sent a quick smile back to Patricia, who motioned with her hands for Alicia to go.

Dante pulled her in to his side and Alicia felt as if she'd have preferred to stay on the periphery and not in the centre of this man's orbit. Everyone was looking at her like a specimen under a microscope. Especially Buchanen, a rotund man with penetrating eyes.

'Everyone, I'd like to introduce you to Alicia Parker…'

Alicia nodded and smiled hello as people came forward and were introduced. She hadn't imagined some of the funny looks Dante had received, as if indeed people were somewhat surprised that he'd turned up with someone on his arm. And for a treacherous split second she felt a kinship, as if they were in this together. His hand stayed on or near the middle of her back, sending little electric shocks up and down her spine.

When they sat down for dinner Dante had to let Alicia go and he didn't want to. That moment when he'd pulled her in to his side in the drawing room, she'd looked like a deer caught in the headlights, but after a few minutes she'd relaxed into the situation and had chatted easily. In fact, she'd been so at ease that it had distracted him from his own conversation. They'd got separated as soon as they'd walked in and never before had he had the sensation of wanting to keep a woman close—foolish thoughts again, he'd reasoned to himself. He had to keep tabs on her; wasn't that why she was here in the first place…and to sate his libido?

And then, on the way into dinner, Patricia O'Brien had come and squeezed his hand, saying *sotto voce,* 'She seems like a *lovely* girl.'

He hadn't expected this. He didn't know what he'd really expected but it hadn't been this. She was sitting away from him by a few seats, beside Derek, who was obviously smitten. And, even though Derek was a good twenty years his senior, Dante felt like plucking Alicia bodily from her chair and placing her next to him. He wouldn't put it past her to try and seduce his old friend, and the thought made him sick. He forced himself to look away.

Dante's English right-hand man hadn't been able to come this week so had sent his assistant instead; Jeremy Gore-Black. He was seated next to Dante now and while he had been looking forward to catching up on some vital information, the man's monotone voice was rapidly making Dante more and more irritable.

Alicia sent up silent thanks that she was seated next to someone as gregarious as Derek O'Brien, who was regaling the small audience with hilarious stories. It wasn't hard to smile and look happy, at ease. But she was very aware of Dante a few seats away, aware of his movements, his hands, his head as it inclined towards the person he was talking to.

'Hey…Alicia, wasn't it?'

Alicia nodded and turned to the American on her other side. He was a young man called Brown, if she remembered correctly from the brief recent introduction, Buchanen's assistant. She was immediately aware of trying to make a good impression, even though his eyes weren't meeting hers and he was obviously looking for her pretty much non-existent cleavage. She almost felt like apologizing. Until he looked up, smiled slimily and said, 'So what's a nice girl like you doing in a place like this?'

'I…' Suddenly Alicia was very aware that his question had dropped into a temporary lull in the conversation and everyone seemed to be listening.

'Well…I'm here on the kind invitation of Dante.' She sent what she hoped was a suitably loving smile to him, but it felt forced and he looked dark and unreadable. The man was oblivious to the silence.

'And what exactly do you do, then? Do you have a career?'

All Alicia's hackles rose. His arrogant tone said that he expected she did anything *but* work. 'Yes—' she just managed to sound civil '—I'm a qualified nurse and midwife actually.'

Dante cut in then, surprising her, and surprising himself for feeling that he wanted to defend her. 'She's recently returned from a year spent in Africa.'

An audible gasp went up when she answered some questions as to where she'd been. Even Dante had to admit surprise. The place she mentioned was notoriously volatile and Dante wondered what her experiences had been.

After a moment's hush, suddenly the conversation resumed at breakneck speed and Alicia found herself answering questions all around her. She caught Patricia's eye at one stage and she winked at her conspiratorially, as if to say, Well done. And

Alicia did feel a little dart of something like triumph, as if she'd passed some kind of test.

That night, when the after dinner drinks had broken up, Alicia and Dante climbed the stairs to their bedrooms, which were slightly separate from everyone else's. Alicia stopped at her door and couldn't stop a tremor from starting in her legs. What if he—?

'You obviously handled Buchanen well earlier. He can be a difficult man to deal with.'

She whirled around and tried to gauge his expression but it was hidden in the shadows of the hall. He certainly didn't look ready to ravish her. He looked remote and utterly unperturbed. And why did she feel so confused about that? She tried to remember what he'd said—*he* had no problem keeping his hands off her, and she...she felt like some kind of lust-crazed schoolgirl.

Dante looked at her, remembering how Buchanen had cornered her after the dinner and how, despite his best efforts, he hadn't been able to intervene. But when he had come over, Buchanen had been laughing heartily and was obviously finding Alicia to be quite inoffensive. Why should it surprise him that she'd handled Buchanen so well? After all, wasn't this exactly what he'd wanted?

Alicia unconsciously lifted her chin. 'Funnily enough, Tom told me that his wife also trained as a nurse, so we had a lot in common, actually.'

Dante raised an incredulous brow. *Tom?* Who would have thought? He recalled the way she'd been so warm, and then the way she'd shut down when he'd interrupted them. The way that had made him feel. His voice felt tight. 'Just watch that you don't lead him on to thinking you've got more to offer than just conversation.'

Alicia bit back a shocked gasp but hit back. 'God forbid. I suppose as your *partner* I'm going to have to get used to people thinking I'm some vacuous arm orna—'

His hand snaked out in a heartbeat and wrapped itself around the back of her neck, fingers twisting strands of her hair and tugging. 'Ah, ah, Alicia, no need to go for the low blow.'

She held her head stiff. She *hated* him. Hated him for being the reason that she stood here now, a mass of quivering confusion and swirling feelings. 'What can I say; you bring out the worst in me.'

He abruptly released her and she nearly staggered back, she had held herself so stiff under his hand.

'I had no idea you worked in that place.'

She wanted to curl inwards; her lower back throbbed as if her pain was tangible.

Dante saw the shutters come down and wondered again what had happened to her. This aspect of Alicia he hadn't counted on. And certainly not the uncomfortable contradictions it threw up.

She forced a nonchalant shrug. 'You never asked.' He opened his mouth and she spoke quickly. 'Actually, if you don't mind, I'd prefer not to talk about it.'

He inclined his head and for a split second she saw a flash of something in his eyes—some flame, or fire—and her heart beat quickly in response, but then it was gone.

He stepped back, hands in his pockets. 'We're conducting our meetings in the Villa Monastero in Varenna, which is directly across the lake. Boats will be taking us back and forth every day. You should come over with Patricia, meet us for lunch. Tomorrow is the only day we'll work till evening, after that it'll be just the mornings with the afternoons free for sightseeing. A boat will be at your disposal.'

'O…OK.' Her head swirled again with the enormity of being here with him amidst all this wealth and luxury that seemed to come so naturally.

'Goodnight, Alicia.'

'Goodnight,' she said faintly, and watched him go into his room without a backward glance. She leant back on the closed door of her own room, the moon outside shedding the only light. Damn the man. She had a strong suspicion—a feeling—that she was being lulled into a false sense of security.

But that night, with the knowledge that he lay only feet away, possibly naked, Alicia hardly slept a wink. And made sure to watch from her window in the morning until a certain tall, dark figure had leapt aboard one of the two launches and left for the ornate white villa visible through the haze across the lake. Only then did she go downstairs. And was it her fanciful imagination or had he looked up to her window just as the launch had been pulling away?

That evening, as his boat approached the shore and the wooden walkway that led up to his villa, Dante's blood boiled. Alicia hadn't come over to meet them for lunch. Neither had Patricia, a reasonable voice pointed out. And they'd actually only stopped in the end for half an hour, but still…he'd found himself distracted. Which was not normal for him. He didn't like not knowing what she was up to. He told himself it was because he didn't trust her. He sprang down on to the stones from the walkway, he could see shapes on the terrace ahead of him.

The boats were back. Alicia felt her heart quicken. Patricia's light conversation made it easy to tune out a little and she was aware of footsteps crunching on the stones coming closer and closer. Alicia could feel her breath shorten. She'd wanted to go over to the Villa Monastero for lunch, not wanting to give Dante any excuse for further condemnation, but Patricia had insisted on doing some sightseeing, telling her that the men would never notice their absence and that Dante had probably only been courteous in extending the invitation. With no means of contacting him, she'd felt very keenly that he'd misinterpret her actions as being rebellious in some way.

'Ah, Dante, there you are.' Patricia rose gracefully to greet Dante with a kiss on both cheeks. 'Your lovely Alicia has been the most charming company all day.'

'Has she indeed?'

Alicia stood too, aware that it was only she who heard the hard inflection in his voice. Buchanen and the others were arriving behind them, Derek coming to greet his wife also. Alicia was dismayed by Dante's autocratic manner, the light in his eyes, so that when he reached for her and pulled her in tight against him he caught her unawares.

His voice was low, intimate. 'I missed you, my love. You were supposed to come and meet us for lunch…' He caught a tendril of hair and twisted it around one finger and tugged gently. 'Playing games, Alicia?'

She shook her head, mesmerized by his eyes. And then some measure of sanity returned with the hubbub around them, with the knowledge that he was merely making it look authentic.

'No, Dante. I didn't realize that it had been an order. I don't respond well to orders.' Her mouth was set in a mutinous line and Dante had one clear desire, one way to eradicate the irritation in his blood.

The kiss was harsh, all consuming. And brief, but not brief enough to stop Alicia's pulse soaring or her cheeks flushing.

He stopped and lifted his head. All she could see was dark eyes, a dark face, a cruel smile. It was time to make his intentions clear. 'Then take this how you want—by the end of this week we are going to be lovers.'

'Never,' she breathed immediately with self-protecting swiftness, with horror at his calm assurance. 'Absolutely no way.'

She shook her head, even as her blood sizzled at his nearness. She tried to push free but it was futile against his strength. Eventually he let her go and only the wall at her back kept her from falling.

His eyes flickered down over her silk button down dress, her loose hair and plain earrings. 'You're dressed fine for dinner; stay here and enjoy an aperitif, we'll be down in half an hour.' And, with another swift, devastating kiss, he walked away and Alicia realized that everyone had left. She hadn't even noticed. She turned around and the two launches bobbed with what seemed to be blissful unconcern on the gently lapping waters.

* * *

By the last evening of the week Alicia was a bag of nerves. This situation, which had started out as a result of her assumption that he was the father of Mel's baby, had morphed into something else entirely. Something that had nothing to do with outside influences—something between them. Uniquely. And Alicia had nowhere to turn. Melanie was being cared for, was thriving in the new house with Paolo, who appeared to be the devoted fiancé. Yet that had an awful tendency of slipping from her mind completely, so consumed was she by this man. So consumed had she become, after a week of intimate looks, physical contact, but, as yet…no move to take her to bed.

And the awful thing was, it was all she could think about.

She looked at him now as he drove his car into the small nearby town. Behind them were a couple of luxurious people carriers conveying the guests. The breeze barely ruffled her hair and he drove with sure controlled mastery, those long fingers resting on the gear stick, very close to her leg. They were on their way to have dinner in that same hotel that she'd seen him emerge from only a week ago. And tomorrow they would travel to Cape Town.

She cast him a look and couldn't keep it in any longer—what she'd found out earlier in a conversation with Patricia. Guilt clawed at her *again,* an annoyingly frequent emotion with this man.

'Why didn't you tell me what your plane was really being used for when it brought the clothes? I had no idea that it was bringing children from the orphanage in Milan to the lake for water sports.'

He didn't turn to look at her and was silent for a long time. His jaw clenched and a muscle pulsed under the skin.

'Dante—'

'I heard you.'

'So…why?'

He flicked her a glance and then looked back to the road. 'I didn't tell you because it's none of your business what I use my aeroplane for.'

Hurt struck her with the precision of a tiny arrow. 'I know. But I just…I wish you'd told me, that's all.' Her hands twisted in her lap.

He hated the fact that she had found out. It made him feel absurdly weak…exposed. He cast her a look and arched a brow. 'Spare me the fake interest. The others might be taken in by the selfless aid nurse but I've no doubt you had an agenda. No doubt a man must have been involved—a rich doctor, perhaps? What happened—did it go sour? Is that why you came home and you and your sister schemed to make the best of a bad situation?' he queried idly.

Alicia sucked in a breath. It was on the one hand so near to the truth and on the other so far removed from the truth that she saw spots appear before her eyes. Her anger, for once wasn't hot and tumultuous; it was icy-cold and far stronger.

She turned to face him. 'I take back what I said, for trying to be polite.' She waved an agitated hand. 'No doubt your *apparent philanthropy* is a highly calculated move to endear you to the public. Because, if you didn't at least do that, wouldn't you just be another rags to riches story? Another of the idle *nouveau riche*? No doubt your action gets you major kudos in our politically correct world. Especially here, with people you need to impress…'

The only sign that she'd got to him was his hands clenching on the steering wheel until his knuckles turned white. And stupidly, she was already regretting her words; she knew it was a cheap shot. Patricia had waxed lyrical for nearly an hour earlier, telling her how involved Dante was with the street kids and orphans usually overseeing their activities himself, and that he was patron of numerous charities for street kids in nearly every city in Italy.

His voice when he spoke sent shivers of fear down her spine. 'You're right in one aspect Alicia.'

'I am?' she said hesitantly, all bravado gone.

'Yes.' He sent her a smile and it turned her blood cold. A large brown hand snaked out and gripped her bare thigh, shoving her skirt up roughly. Her immediate reaction was to take his hand off her leg; its effect had been violent. But he pushed her hand away easily.

He still drove, his concentration not gone for a second as that hand inched higher and higher. Alicia tried to clench her legs close together, but her instinct was to relax them. His hand was so high now that he grazed her panties and Alicia had to close her eyes at the awful wantonness of the picture she must present, and at the way she could feel herself start to throb down there. She gripped his wrist but that was worse, she could feel his pulse, his hair roughened skin.

Without her even realizing it, he'd pulled in to park outside the hotel with a smooth move and, before anyone approached them, he leant over, cupping her sex properly, intimately. He was dark, smouldering, intense. She couldn't speak. She was on fire and he knew it.

'Yes. You are right…all we need to focus on is *this*. Who cares what we do, what we are?'

She opened her mouth to speak, to say, Stop, I do care, and he halted her words by meeting her lips with a devastating kiss that was so incendiary that she could feel herself reacting, shamelessly wanting to push into his hand in a totally instinctive move. He pulled back, his eyes glittering, a mocking triumphant smile on his face. She coloured in shame, a vivid recollection of only a week before, the way he'd left that woman on the nearby steps coming back to taunt her.

'And don't even try to deny it any more. This is why you're here, why I'm even indulging you or your sister at all.'

At that moment Alicia knew that she was in more trouble than she'd ever been in her entire life and that this man had the power to hurt her in a way that made anything that had gone before seem like nothing more than a teenage crush.

CHAPTER ELEVEN

ON THE DRIVE back to the villa after dinner, which seemed to have passed in an indecently short amount of time, there was no conversation. They had stayed for coffee after dessert and when everyone else, in various states of inebriation decided to go to the club downstairs, Dante had taken Alicia's hand and led her outside.

And now Alicia sat like a statue: fear, a little bit of loathing, largely directed at herself and aching desire all warring in her body.

They pulled up on the gravel and Julieta—lovely, kind Julieta—appeared in the doorway to greet them. Alicia gave her a kiss goodnight and wanted to cling on to her for dear life. But Dante took her hand again and led her to the stairs. She stumbled at the bottom step in her heels and Dante barely changed pace as he caught her under her legs and lifted her up into his arms. Still no words. She looked at his face, which was impassive, carved from stone. Remote. Cold. How could they do this with so little warmth or affection?

He strode confidently past her door and reality sank in. His door was shut behind them and then she was on her feet, breathless, as if she'd been the one carrying him in what seemed like a mere second. She backed away and made for her own adjoining door but he caught her back easily.

'No, you don't.'

Alicia arched away from him as much as she could within the steel band of his arms. 'I don't want to do this; I won't do this.'

He didn't answer, making him seem even more dark and dangerous. Remote. When he lowered his head to hers she twisted hers away and, with more than a touch of ruthlessness, he turned her head back to his. Her whole body was stiff, fighting the urge to sink, and melt.

'No...' She struggled again, fruitlessly.

He bent his head to hers and caught her mouth. The sensation was shocking and Alicia tore her head away again, every ounce of her strength going into this struggle, this fight. But Dante was utterly remorseless. With her head turned away, he pressed his mouth against her neck. Her fists beat against his chest and made absolutely no impact. Without force, he merely twisted one arm back behind her, bringing her breasts into tight proximity to his broad chest. There was something untamed about him that called to some deep, dark part of her.

The feel of his arousal against her soft flesh was too much, pushing her over the edge. It started a drum beat of desire in her blood. She could feel the battle being lost, her limbs shaking with the effort it took to resist when she didn't want to. His mouth descended into the valley exposed by her wrapover top. Her free hand was on his shoulder, it moved to his head, his hair... but instead of pulling him away, as she'd fully intended, that hand caught in the short, silky dark strands and clung on. Then his hand gripped one buttock and he pulled her against him in a move that made her gasp with its earthy sensuality, its urgency. She felt a force flood her entire body and an unbelievably strong urge to connect in the most intimate way with this man. And she knew, at that moment, that *he knew* she'd tacitly acquiesced.

Alicia's legs nearly buckled as she swayed. He caught her, lifting her again, and brought her over to the bed, where he put her down on her feet. This time, when he bent his head, she didn't move, couldn't fight. Angry with him for making her feel so weak and with herself for this unwanted response, she kissed him back with passion and anger, matching him, their mouths clinging, tongues searching and stroking with heady intimacy.

Her anger emboldened her. Her hands went to his jacket and pushed it from his shoulders, it fell to the floor. He ripped at his bow tie, she heard material tear but it only echoed the sound of her pulse soaring as she watched him open his shirt, to reveal his torso. For a second she couldn't breathe, just taking in the sight of the sheer bronzed magnificence in front of her. Acting on pure impulse, she stretched out her hands and spread them across the wide plane, the light smattering of hair; her eyes followed it down and she saw the bulge just under his belt.

A finger tipped her chin up. 'Undo my belt...and trousers.'

She was shaking as she did as he asked, sliding the belt through the buckle and through the loops until it fell open. Her hand went to the top button; she could already feel the heat of him. Slowly, because she was shaking too much to go quickly, she drew the zip down and her knuckles brushed enticingly against his erection, which pulsed and strained against the material of his briefs. He sucked in a breath above her and, when she looked up, they were the only two people in the world. His eyes glittered down at her. Right now, there was only this.

With jerky impatience Dante brushed her hand away and stepped out of his trousers and briefs, standing in front of her, entirely naked. Bronzed, glistening skin stretched over hard, hard muscles. Something caught Alicia's eye and she instinctively put out a finger to touch—it was a tattoo on his right arm, high up. Some kind of ancient symbol. It looked rough, as if it hadn't been done properly. The air was very still and heavy around them as she traced it with a small finger. Her eyes grew round.

A burst of angry cynicism rushed through Dante and he smiled down at her harshly. 'It was part of my initiation into a gang. Does it excite you?'

Alicia felt sad…for what he must have gone through. She looked up hesitantly and shook her head minutely. She knew he wouldn't appreciate her pity. Even so, she couldn't help asking, 'What does it mean?'

Dante took her finger away and brought it to his mouth, sucking the tip deeply inwards before releasing it again. A spasm of lust gripped her, warring with a scary falling feeling in her chest.

He caught the gleam of something in her eyes and felt something beat in his chest—a warning: *danger, danger…*

He called back that anger, even though it was fast being obliterated by the lust firing his blood. 'It means, *cara,* that I trust no one…'

*And especially not me…*flashed through her head.

But, before she had time to think about it, he had undone the catch at the back of her skirt; it fell to the floor with a swish, and then her top followed equally rapidly. She kicked off her shoes, which lowered her a few precious inches. Dante nudged her back on to the bed. She hadn't looked yet but now she couldn't avoid seeing him—*all* of him. And he looked very aroused. She felt a dart of fear in her belly. What if he was too big for her? And, just as quickly, she felt a rush of liquid desire, moistening her, making her ready to take him. Her own body, a traitor of the worst kind.

He dispensed with her bra and came beside her on one arm, looking his fill. Her breasts seemed to tighten even more, the tips flagrantly aroused, waiting, hungering for his touch, his mouth. As if he read her mind, he passed a palm over one nipple and Alicia shivered. But she exploded into pieces when he bent his head and took it into his mouth, suckling roughly. Her body arched and his hand came around and under her back to pull her close.

Instinctively she stiffened and recoiled as his hand moved down over the still tender skin of her scar. His head came up. 'What the hell is that?'

Before she could say a word or move, he had turned her in to him to inspect what she knew was a large area of puckered pink scar tissue just above her right buttock. She closed her eyes and pushed away from him so violently that he had to let her go. She was glad of the dark. She scooted back up the bed and hugged her arms around herself, knees up. Guilt, fear and self-consciousness all vied in her breast.

He was looking at her…with *pity?* As much as she couldn't bear his censure, she couldn't bear this.

'It's nothing.'

'It's hardly nothing, Alicia; you've got a huge scar on your back. Where did you get it? Is it sore?'

'It's only sore sometimes, if I do too much or anything too physical.'

Dante had a sudden memory of throwing her over his shoulder and winced, guilt rushing through him. Alicia saw it and read it. Her mouth twisted. 'You weren't to know.'

'No,' he said harshly, 'but I didn't need to be so rough.'

Something in his voice inexplicably made her melt inside, made her forget her intention not to tell him anything. 'I…it happened about five months ago. Rebel militia had surrounded the aid camp and were taking pot shots at us. They killed twenty people. The bullet that got me was a ricochet. I'm lucky, it turned out to be little more than a flesh wound…'

Dante had moved off the bed and pulled on his trousers, leaving them open. *Lucky.* He knew that had to be an understatement. She spoke so carefully and precisely that he knew well she was trying to avoid remembering the undoubted horror. If she was telling the truth…something urged him to believe that she was, though…she'd reacted too forcibly to him touching her there.

Alicia's gaze was drawn to where the hair descended in a line to the potent heat of him—the heat that had almost consumed them. She closed her eyes and turned her head in disgust at herself. But she had to focus on him, on the physical, because if she didn't…she would think about the rest. Her hands clenched.

Dante paced close to the bed. She'd been shot. A bullet had passed through her flesh…*Alicia's flesh*…cutting it open. He stopped and felt a curious weakness in his chest for a moment. He looked at her averted profile, her chest moving up and down, her breasts crushed by her knees and arms. He realized then too that she'd said this had happened five months ago…and she'd obviously stayed, hadn't left a dangerous situation…thoughts were shifting around him, in him, and he couldn't stop them.

He sat down on the side of the bed and watched as the colour flooded her cheeks. He ran a finger up and down her arm and saw goosebumps spring up. Even now, he burned for her. He spoke her name without thinking, instinctively. 'Alicia…'

She looked up at him with desperation in her eyes. It shocked him. Her hair was tumbled over her shoulders, her eyes were huge and again the thought of someone shooting at her made him want to gather her up close and never let her go. A maelstrom of emotions ran through him.

'I'm OK. It's fine.'

But she wasn't. Everything was starting to flood back. Images, faces of the dying…the ever present danger. And yet, right now, being here with this man and the power he held over her body and mind scared her witless too.

She could move, get up, leave the room; she knew instinctively that he would let her go. But…this *heat* that vibrated between them wouldn't let her move, as much as she wanted to. As much as it terrified her.

This man had the power to halt all the terrible images that

threatened to flood her mind. She remembered the feeling of safety she'd had in his arms. And, right then, desire surged through her, powerful and so strong—again she had that overwhelming urge to lie with him, *be* with him. She knew she was flirting with a far more dangerous fire in order to obliterate her own pain, even for a short while. She needed to feel *alive,* needed some of this man's potent vibrancy. The fact that she was allowing herself to be seduced yet again... She blocked it out. And she knew, somewhere that she wasn't willing to look at yet, that Raul Carro had never had her so aflame that she couldn't resist.

Before she could lose her nerve, she took her hands away from her breasts and lay down on the bed. And also before she could lose her nerve, in a bold and completely untutored instinctive move, she lifted her hips and slipped her panties off. She lay there naked. She saw the confusion in Dante's eyes, the split second of hesitation before a familiar hardness crossed his face.

Without a word, he stood and slipped his trousers off lean hips again. This time she didn't look down; she looked up and, as Dante came down beside her and lowered his head to hers, she breathed a sigh of relief. This danger was infinitely preferable to being vulnerable in front of him. She twined her arms around his neck, holding him close, revelling in the heat of him, the scent of him and the protective strength of him. Sexual heat combusted all around them, white-hot and illuminating. Within what seemed like minutes they had surpassed where they'd got to before and all that Alicia was aware of was the man who hovered over her, muscles bunched in his arms as he looked down at her.

His hand parted her legs and she had a brief moment of trepidation as she could feel the smooth head of him nudge her slick entrance. As if sensing that fear, Dante stopped for a second, even though never before had he had the urge to drive in so far and so deep that he'd lose himself. He put a hand between them, feeling for himself. Her wetness made him throb; she was so ready. She moaned as his hand moved and he slipped a couple of fingers inside her. She bit her lip and moved her hips slightly against him and then he took his hand away.

'No, *bella,* it's going to be much better than that.'

And, lowering his body, pushing against her, he slid in. Sweat broke out on his brow at the first feel of her tight muscles squeezing around him, holding him so snugly that he didn't even know if he could push in any more, but then he felt her hands on his arms and she tilted her hips and he slid deeper. He bit back a long moan of pure masculine joy and pleasure. No woman had ever felt like this around him. So snug, so tight, so *hot.*

He looked down into Alicia's eyes and they were black pools of want and need. He flexed his bottom and kept sliding in, all the way.

His breathing was harsh and jagged, like hers. Alicia looked up, wide-eyed. She'd never felt so stretched, so full…so full of aching tightening sensations; they were building through her body like a delicious tidal wave of sensation upon sensation. Dante slowly started to move, in and out. He tilted her hips, deepening the penetration even further and Alicia moaned softly, wrapping her legs around his back, as far as they would go.

She pulled his head back down to her, searching for and finding his mouth just as he thrust deep and hit the very heart of her again, and she gasped against his mouth. All her muscles were tensing; she couldn't believe she was so close already, but the waves were building and there was nothing she could do to stop them. Her back arched and she cried out as she exploded into pieces around him. But he wasn't done, not yet…

With long, hard thrusts he kept moving and, although her body was so sensitive for a second that it almost hurt, Alicia could feel herself adjust and start building all over again. She thought to herself: It's not possible…she wouldn't be able to survive another orgasm like it…but Dante had other ideas.

Alicia gripped his arms. Their bodies were slick with sweat, her legs fell from his back as she tensed again. And, just as the wave crested, he lowered his head and caught one nipple in his mouth, sucking fiercely, and Alicia couldn't stop the tremors, even stronger this time from gripping her whole body and turning everything black for a second. The world shifted back into focus just as Dante tensed above her and in her, before his own body spasmed and she felt the pulsating strength of him release deep into her body. And in that moment, as he fell over her in a dead slump, everything suddenly made sense to Alicia. As if she'd lived just for this moment.

After a long minute of their intermingling breaths lengthening and becoming normal again, their frantic heartbeats slowing, Dante finally found the strength to roll off Alicia and lay at her side. He wanted to pull her close, take her hand, and had to clench his fist to stop the impulsive action. Great sex. That was all it was. Great sex had the biological result of inviting feelings of affection, wanting to be close. Even if it had never happened before…or the only time it had happened he'd learnt his lesson never to succumb again and, so far, he'd never met a woman who'd inspired this feeling…until now. Which proved to him that he was right not to trust her an inch.

She was the same—all mercenary women were the same.

He jackknifed off the bed and was about to stand up when sudden cold horror spread through him. He looked back at the woman behind him. Her eyes were closed, her arm was over her face and her shoulders shaking ever so slightly. *Was she crying?* It momentarily diverted him from his very unwelcome revelation.

He reached back and took her arm down. Her eyes remained shut but he could see wetness on her cheeks.

'Alicia.'

She opened her eyes finally and pulled her arm from his hand. She sat up and got off the bed, her face a mask of indifference as she bent and picked up her clothes. Awkwardly pulling on her skirt and holding the rest of her things over her chest, she walked to the door of her bedroom.

Still stunned and surprised at her actions, at the evidence of tears, Dante could only watch. She turned at the door and said huskily, with the slightest catch in her voice, 'Just so you know, as you obviously don't think about such mundane matters, I'm on the pill, so there shouldn't be any consequences of this...' she was obviously searching for words '...*act.*'

And then she slipped through the door and disappeared. How dared she? Dante jumped up, incensed, his male pride bristling, and took a few steps towards the door before stopping himself. The thought of protection or, more to the point, the lack of it was the thing that had made him stop in abject horror. He *never, ever* forgot about protection. He was fanatical about it and, on very rare occasions where he didn't have any and he didn't trust the woman if she told him she was on the pill, he had no qualms about calling a halt to things.

But just now...heat flooded his body and he felt himself becoming aroused again with very little stimulation, at just the *thought* of what had happened...it had not even occurred to him. He grimaced and ran an angry hand through his hair. She had every right to have that tone in her voice if she thought he acted like that on a regular basis.

He turned from the door and went into his shower, stepping under a punishing cold spray. Why had she been crying? His movements stilled. Could it have been because he'd hurt her? But then he remembered that mind-blowing climax; he'd been certain that it had been exactly the same for her—those moans and sighs hadn't been of pain... Still, he had a nasty taste in his mouth as he stepped out and dried off.

Alicia didn't know where she'd had the confidence to get off that bed so coolly, put on her skirt and leave the room without the awful shaking gripping her body. What had just happened to her...was so huge...that she couldn't acknowledge it or dwell on it. She stood under the hot shower, letting the water sluice down over her skin. She didn't even have the energy to wash her hair and had to keep twisting when the water hit a still too sensitive patch of skin. She remembered the feel of his hand on her scar, the vulnerability she'd felt, and hurriedly stopped that train of thought.

She couldn't believe that he hadn't thought of protection and, to be honest, she was surprised that she'd only thought of it in that split second at the door. He seemed like the kind of man who would be concerned about something so fundamental, especially when he'd been so adamant when she'd accused him of fathering Mel's baby. He'd been certain, and only a man who protected himself would be that certain. Not that she'd given him the benefit of the doubt, of course, she had to concede.

And, had he seen her tears? Did he know that he'd moved her to tears with his body? Moved her to tears because she'd never experienced such pure, primal pleasure in her life? Because for the last year she'd cut off an emotional part of herself that she'd thought had been lost for ever. She'd had to, in order to survive.

But just now, here, this man had made her *feel* again. She remonstrated with herself, she'd wanted to feel alive again and now she didn't know if she could take it. She'd played a game that she'd thought, stupidly, she'd be sophisticated enough to handle but it had shown her nothing but her weakness.

Alicia towelled herself quickly and then climbed under the covers of her bed. Her body still throbbed and pulsed in secret places. And, even though she'd just washed, the scent of him lingered.

Before she fell into a sleep of physical exhaustion, her head in turmoil, the lingering thought remained, *How was it possible that this man, above any other had given her back something so precious?* When another man, just like him, had taken it away…

CHAPTER TWELVE

'I'VE booked everyone into a small boutique hotel for the next two weeks. It's owned by a friend of mine from France. He would have been here to host us himself but he and his wife are having another baby any day now.'

'You're talking about Xavier Salgado-Lezille?'

Dante nodded at Derek O'Brien, who shook his head mock mournfully. 'They had twins only a couple of years ago...' He pretended to shudder and winked at Alicia who forced a smile. 'I'm glad ours are all grown up, that's all I can say.'

His wife laughed and rolled her eyes. 'Don't be scaring them, Derek. You are the quintessential doting father of four girls; you're fooling no one.'

Then she said in an aside to Alicia, 'All the girls are busy this summer working or getting ready for college; otherwise they'd be here in force to support us...'

Alicia murmured something polite and looked out of the window of the people carrier and swallowed an inexplicable lump in her throat, wishing she could tune out the conversation, hating feeling so emotional. She couldn't—wouldn't—meet Dante's laser like gaze opposite her and wished she'd worn her sunglasses.

They were on the way to their Cape Town hotel which was in the trendy area of Camps Bay, near the beach. And she'd finally understood what Dante had been talking about when he'd mentioned the media interest—the airport in Milan had been mobbed. She'd even recognised the faces of the reporter and photographer who she had contacted that awful first night. And, when they'd arrived into Cape Town, another scrum had been waiting for them. She'd been too scared to do anything but cling on to Dante's hand as he had guided them through the crush, ignoring questions. Alicia had felt as if they'd see through her in a second. That someone would call out, *What on earth are you doing with her?*

She could feel some of the tension ebbing away already as they passed through the pretty city, and she'd been so relieved to find them sharing Dante's plane with Derek and chatty Patricia. But she knew there wouldn't be much respite as he had said they would be sharing a room here. She'd managed to avoid any meaningful contact today but had caught Dante's eye several times and, along with the inevitable heat flaring between them, had been a look—a look that said she wouldn't escape.

As soon as they arrived, Alex, Dante's assistant, appeared, apologized to Alicia and commandeered Dante for the rest of the day to set things up. Alicia faked her dismay and Dante gave her a very pointed look as he walked away. She breathed a huge sigh of relief and went to explore their suite. The luggage had been delivered already and Alicia shook her head wryly. This was what extreme wealth did. The suite was huge, with a deck balcony that looked out over the beautiful beaches of Camps Bay. It was simply stunning.

Alicia felt quite emotional as she took it in, thinking about the difference between here and where she'd been up until a few weeks ago.

She busied herself unpacking and decided a couple of hours later to go downstairs and check out the surroundings. She was standing at the reception desk waiting for a map when she heard a voice behind her and it sent shivers of recognition down her spine.

'Well, well, well, if it isn't little Alicia Parker. Isn't the world the smallest place?'

Alicia turned around slowly. A tall woman stood behind her, long black glossy hair, an over-made-up face, hard blue eyes. Her stomach fell. Of all the places and all the people. She couldn't even pretend to smile—what was the point? There was no love lost between them. As student nurses and then nurses together, this woman had fought a continuous battle with Alicia, whether it had been in exams or going for jobs.

Alicia had had to give up trying to be friendly and make her see that she wasn't interested in being her number one competitor. And then, unbeknownst to Alicia until far too late, it had finally culminated in the ultimate competition—for a man— except in the end they'd both suffered equally.

'Serena Cox.'

The woman smiled nastily and gestured to a small rotund man at the other end of the reception desk. 'Serena Gore-Black now. I'm married to Jeremy.'

Alicia looked at the man fleetingly. She knew he was from Dante's company in London. She'd exchanged pleasantries with him at Lake Como; they'd talked a bit about Melanie but Alicia had been careful not to mention Paolo and he seemed not to have heard anything. She couldn't believe this twist of fateful coincidence; it was too cruel.

'That's…nice.'

'And you're here with?'

'Dante D'Aquanni.'

Alicia got no satisfaction from the momentary flash of undisguised envy in Serena's eyes.

'Really?' Serena's eyes did a once over, taking in Alicia's understated, yet obviously expensive clothes. 'You've done well for yourself, haven't you?'

Alicia smiled tightly. 'I really should be getting back—'

Serena's husband came over to join them. He smiled at Alicia and she had to smile back. He seemed like a nice man, she thought again, apart from his wife.

'Darling, I can't believe I've run into Alicia Parker…or should I say D'Aquanni?'

Alicia turned puce. 'No, it's Parker.' *As if!*

'I'm sure it is.' There was a gleam of triumph in Serena's eyes. She looked at her husband. 'We used to work together in the Royal a few years ago.'

Jeremy made a polite noise and Alicia fairly sagged back against the desk when they finally walked away. This was not good. Serena was a prize mischief-maker. And she knew far too much.

When Dante returned to the suite that evening, Alicia was ready and waiting for dinner. He barely cast her a quick glance as he shed his clothes on the way to the shower. She looked away hurriedly and went to stand out on the balcony. It was artfully secluded and kept private from prying eyes.

When she heard him emerge behind her she didn't turn around, not wanting to see him getting dressed, but what was she going to do tonight? She felt panic rise. Because if he so much as looked at her she was going to find it hard to resist. A treacherous sexual tension had been building inside her all day, despite her head willing her body to behave.

Dante buttoned his shirt and looked at Alicia's slim, taut back. The momentary memory of that scar just above her right buttock made him feel curiously protective. For a second. And then he quashed it. For all he knew, he told himself with something that felt like dogged obstinacy, it *could* just be a story… He hadn't forgotten the way she'd so coolly laid herself bare for him just afterwards. It had jarred with him then, and jarred again now.

She wore a cream silk dress, it was tight fitting and ruched, emphasising her curves, and suddenly desire was heavy and potent in him. He wanted to stop dressing and go over there, take her hair down from its neat chignon, pull down that zip… His hands stilled for a second, desire coming close to winning out, but then he had to stop. They couldn't. There would be plenty of time later.

Alicia felt Dante's eyes boring into her back. She still fought against turning around, too scared to look, and then the spell was broken by his curt voice.

'I'm ready, let's go.'

She turned around and was glad to see him dressed. She walked in and picked up a wrap. His eyes drifted down from her face and over her body, which heated up with awful predictability.

'Am I OK?'

'You'll do.'

Well, there was a backhanded compliment if ever there was one, she thought, bringing her back to earth with a bump.

They walked to the door and Dante was about to allow her to precede him when he stopped her and looked very pointedly at her feet. She looked down, confused, and saw that she'd forgotten to put her shoes on. He had her head in a complete tizzy.

'Sorry…' She blushed furiously and found them, wincing a little as she put them on. They were cream silk, a slightly darker shade than the dress, with little jewels on the front. Killer heels. And they hurt like hell. When she stood up Dante had to suck in a breath, they pushed everything out that was meant to tease and entice a man. Her bottom and her breasts. He'd never noticed before how erotic it could be to watch a woman put on shoes.

She walked carefully towards him and he shut the door again for a second. She looked at him warily, 'What…? We're going to be late.'

He pulled her in to him, the heels gave her added height, bringing her closer to his mouth.

Bending down and capturing her head with a hand in her hair, he kissed her. Alicia put her hand on his wrist and felt his pulse, his skin. His mouth moved over hers and all of last night's passion and force came back instantly. She moaned, half in despair and half in heat-induced lust as she swayed in towards him and her mouth opened, and he took full advantage. Just as she'd feared, her iron-clad intentions were not so iron-clad in the forcefield of this man.

It was the burning feel of his arousal against her that woke her up and she pulled back with effort. She knew her eyes must be bright, her cheeks flushed. She felt hot and tingly all over.

'Dante…I'm not going to sleep with you again. This wasn't part of the arrangement.' There was some kind of desperation in her voice. 'Please. I'm just here as your hostess to make things look good.'

Dante shook his head, his eyes flashing. 'The arrangement has changed. You're here now as my partner in every sense of the word. Why would you want to deny yourself this?' He placed a hand on her heart, just below her breasts; it was thumping out of control.

He shook his head again. 'It's just sex, *cara*—amazing sex. We don't have to like each other…or respect each other in the morning.'

Inside, Alicia shrivelled up and died at his cynical words. At least Raul Carro had couched his desire in a fake haze of love. Dante pulled no punches and, in a way, she should be grateful for that, but still she was determined to hold out in whatever way possible, because she could not endure or cope with the kind of pleasure he could wring from her body again.

Tight-lipped, she reached past him and opened the door, stepping out into the corridor. He followed and looked at her back, walking away from him. It had been on the tip of his tongue a few minutes ago to say something about last night, about not using protection, but now he knew he couldn't. He wasn't ready to face up to that fact yet himself—that she'd made him so hot that he'd forgotten—and, if he explained, he didn't want her to read anything into it. And she would. Because she was a gold-digger and arch manipulator.

So why did that sound a little hollow to his ears now? He took in her rigid profile as they descended in the lift and reached for her hand. She looked up at him warily and he had a sudden picture of her about to walk out of the door in bare feet. The expression in her eyes now and *that* made him feel very strange. The bell pinged and they walked out.

The few wives and partners and children had also arrived today but when they emerged out to the dining area—on a decked platform which was somehow amazingly suspended over the beach—Alicia was still taken aback. There now seemed to be way more people and children running around in between legs and feet. It was a far cry from the cosy, protected intimacy of Lake Como.

And, almost immediately, she caught Serena's eye in the distance. The woman gave her another cold once-over and took in the man who still held her hand. Alicia's tightened on his instinctively, as if to protect herself from harm. Dante looked down. 'What is it?'

She looked up and shook her head. 'Nothing…nothing.'

The dinner itself was somewhat chaotic but quite pleasant. Patricia came and found her and sat down as they had their coffee as people were breaking away from the table. 'Well, my dear, quite a difference from last week, isn't it?'

Alicia smiled and nodded. Some of the crowd had gone into the bar behind them, which was open at one end to the warm night air. With dim lighting and soft jazz playing, it was all very seductive. Alicia sighed deeply and, bizarrely, felt a little relaxed.

'So, if you don't mind me asking, how *did* you two meet?' Patricia looked at Alicia with her intelligent and kind gaze.

Alicia felt such a fraud. She searched for some way to fudge the truth. 'Well, it wasn't exactly conventional.'

Patricia smiled a conspiratorial smile. 'With a man like Dante I'm not surprised, my dear. He's not exactly the conventional type, is he?'

Alicia's eyes snagged on the man with deadly inevitability. He stood in the bar in a throng of people, proud and resplendent in dark trousers and a light shirt. No, he wasn't. He was complex and hard, yet in bed, or when he kissed her… Her heart clenched so tight for a moment that she had to close her eyes briefly. She finally regained control and looked back at Patricia and shook her head. 'No, he's not.'

'I'd like to tell you something, Alicia, and I'm sure Derek won't mind…'

Alicia looked at her curiously, glad to have the focus taken off her and Dante.

'If it wasn't for this merger, Derek's company might have folded.'

Alicia frowned. 'What do you mean?'

Patricia shuddered slightly. 'I mean that he almost went bankrupt. His company took a big hit in recent years with the downturn in the property market and he was too proud to accept help…'

She looked at Alicia and couldn't hide the glimmer of moisture in her eyes. Alicia's heart went out to her as she touched her arm. She automatically thought of their four daughters, the joviality that Derek obviously hid behind.

'Derek helped Dante once a long time ago, gave him his first big contract, because he was too busy himself to take it on. And Dante's never forgotten. Derek isn't investing half of what Dante and Buchanen are in this merger, but Dante doesn't care. He's carrying the deficit. And, with this merger, he's going to be able to give Derek back his company…'

Alicia reeled with that knowledge. 'I had no idea.'

The older woman smiled a watery smile. 'Oh, I'm not surprised, my dear. Dante would want to protect Derek's reputation at all costs.'

Patricia laughed then. 'Listen to me! Let's go and join the men; some of those women are looking far too interested in Dante's considerable charms and, while I don't doubt he's only got eyes for you, let's not give them a chance to knock you off your pedestal.'

Alicia stood up, still reeling and thought hysterically, *Knock her off her pedestal?* She'd started out from near enough the gutter as far as Dante was concerned, so where would she have to fall to?

In love...

That stopped her in her tracks. And she only moved forward after a second—jerkily. No way. It couldn't be possible.

CHAPTER THIRTEEN

'I'M GOING to go up to bed.'

Dante's jaw clenched and for a moment he looked as if he was going to order her to stay. But then he just nodded.

'Thank you.'

The fact that she'd thanked him, as if he were some kind of gaoler, rankled with him. She turned to go making her way through the crush, and Dante only registered then how pale her face had been, her features tight. He remembered her deep, heavy sleep that first night in the villa, the fact that she'd been shot...and a whole host of unwelcome feelings started to flood through him.

Alicia opened the door to the suite with unchecked relief. Her head throbbed mercilessly and she kicked off her shoes, gasping in pain as she did. Her heels were bleeding. She winced as she looked down. Haste made her clumsy; she wanted to be in bed and asleep by the time Dante came in. She couldn't bear it if he touched her tonight, not after what had just sprung to life in her mind, her heart. Patricia's words resounded in her head—the truth revealed of the depth of Dante's loyalty to a friend in need.

Could she possibly, fatalistically, be falling in love with the man? And if she was, had none of the pain she'd endured with Raul Carro taught her anything?

Despair flooded through her. She felt tears of self-pity prick her eyes as she tended her feet and took some aspirin for her headache. Splashing cold water on her face, she looked at herself sternly in the mirror. She had no reason to feel sorry for herself. She shut her eyes. If all she had to worry about was whether or not she was falling in love with Dante, then she wasn't doing too badly.

She climbed into bed, feeling very alone. Melanie was in London with Paolo. Alicia had called her earlier and she'd heard about the first scan with Dr Hardy that morning which had shown that everything was OK and progressing normally. So when Alicia couldn't stop the tears and they fell unchecked down her cheeks, she told herself it was because she was so happy for Melanie. And that it had nothing to do with the past and the role she'd played in it. Or for herself now.

Dante came into the room quietly. He'd tried to get away from the bar ages ago but had been constantly stopped on his way out. As soon as Alicia had left him alone, a steady stream of women had accosted him. It always amazed him, but didn't surprise him, how blatant they were under the noses of their own husbands and partners. And somehow, knowing Alicia was there, they were even more pushy, as if bringing a woman was throwing down some kind of provocative gauntlet.

He came and stood close to the bed. Alicia was asleep on her back, her hair in disarray around her head. She looked innocently childlike in silk pyjamas, buttoned up almost to her neck. Something like anger flooded him. Why wasn't she sleeping naked? Why wasn't she waiting up—waiting for him? His eyes travelled down and he frowned. She'd thrown off the cover and her foot peeped out; he could see a ring of what looked like dried blood around the heel. Had that been from the shoes?

He straightened and his expression became stony as he recalled what someone had just told him. While he trusted that person about as much as he trusted Alicia, he had to admit that what he'd heard probably was the truth and he didn't want to acknowledge the ridiculous disappointment he felt. Instead he let the anger rise. Alicia was going to prove a liability after all...

When Alicia woke the following morning her first feeling was of uneasiness. She opened her eyes, assessing her surroundings in a second. The bed was empty beside her. Relief flooded her; she'd survived the night.

'No need to look so happy with yourself.'

She flinched and her head turned to find where Dante's voice had come from. He sat on the balcony, a table set up for breakfast.

'Come join me; it's beautiful out here.'

Why didn't she trust his easy invitation? But she couldn't stay in bed either and he was dressed so that made her feel a little more relaxed. She pulled a hotel robe around her pyjamas and he noted her action with a dry look as she came out.

'I think I can control myself; you don't have to cover yourself up like a yeti.'

She scowled at him and helped herself to some fruit and a croissant.

He sat back, watching her, and sipped at his coffee. She avoided his gaze and looked out over the amazing view—the clear blue sky, clean beach and blue water that rushed in in foaming waves. And, as he watched her he had to acknowledge again what a duplicitous nature her innocent looking face hid. But then what had he expected?

'I had an interesting talk last night with an old colleague of yours.' Dante's tone was idle, bored even.

Immediately Alicia's blood turned to ice in her veins and her hand stilled on the way to her mouth with a glass of juice. She dropped it back down with a clatter and looked at Dante reluctantly, her chin coming up unconsciously. Serena obviously hadn't wasted any time.

'And? Come on out with it, you're obviously dying to tell me.' Fury and disdain sparked in her eyes and Dante felt a little nonplussed; shouldn't he be the one looking at her disdainfully?

'Serena Gore-Black, Jeremy's wife…I didn't realize you knew him.'

Alicia was defensive. 'I don't. I only found out yesterday that Serena was married to him when I saw her here.'

Her head went into a spin, trying to figure what she might have said; she wouldn't put it past Serena to have given him all the gory details. 'We worked in the same hospital a couple of years ago. But please, do tell me what scintillating titbit of half information she passed on to you.'

Half information.

Dante frowned slightly, the overbearing woman had had the same zealous look in her eye as all the other women. Come to think of it, the only woman who didn't look at him like that was Alicia. It made his voice harsh. 'Well, you obviously already know—she told me about your adulterous affair with Dr Raul… What was the name?'

So she had done it. Pain sliced through Alicia, even though she tried to deny it, and guilt, clawing at her insides. That would never go. She spoke faintly. 'Carro…Dr Raul Carro.'

'Was he the reason you went to Africa?'

She looked at him for a long moment, something pained in her eyes, and then nodded slowly. She could well imagine that Dante assumed that he had gone too and that she had followed him there. And Carro *had* ended up there…so what was the point of trying to put him straight when he so obviously wanted to think the worst?

After all, he had been a big part of her reason for going. But it had been to get as far away as possible, disgusted and sickened by what had happened. By the fact that she'd fallen for someone so amoral.

Her obvious confirmation of the story made something weigh Dante's chest down. He leaned forward. 'So you don't deny you had an affair with a married man, who had a wife and four children at home in Spain?'

Alicia got up jerkily, unable to bear it, and stood at the railing, her hands gripping it. After a second she turned around, a wild look in her eyes as she fixed them on Dante.

'No. No, I can't deny it. I had an affair with a married man. There, are you happy? You can just lump this on top of the gold-digger label. There. Does that please you? All the justification you might need to feel better about yourself. I'm a bad, wicked woman. A gold-digger and a husband-stealer.'

Dante stood too and came close, his features livid, her barb about justification cutting far too close to the bone. 'Well, let's just say that it doesn't surprise me. But what the hell do I care anyway? You mean nothing to me, and as for your conniving sister—'

Alicia's hand came out of nowhere and cracked across Dante's cheek. Too shocked to take in what she'd just done, she said very shakily, 'Don't you *ever* mention my sister like that again. She's had enough of your unfair censure and it's entirely your fault that she ended up in hospital in the first place.'

Heat and anger and passion simmered between them like a visible force. With an inarticulate sound and Alicia's livid hand print across one cheek, he hauled her into his arms and drove his mouth down on to hers with punishing force. Bending her back, literally to his will.

With some tiny piece of sanity left to her, Alicia broke her mouth away from his and tried to arch away. 'Dante no—' *Not like this.* The shock was beginning to hit her at what she'd just done—the fact that she'd *hit* him. She'd never struck another living soul in her life.

'Dante, yes.'

Ruthless and determined to get payback, to punish her, he pulled Alicia in to him even tighter and fused his mouth to hers. At the moment their lips touched again the anger that Alicia had been clinging on to fell away like a flimsy wall. Her desire which had been simmering, burst out of control and again that treacherous, all consuming need flooded every part of her.

Dante pulled back after a long moment, his hands encircled Alicia's back, holding her captive. Her cheeks were pink, beads of sweat on her brow, a tendril of hair clung to her cheek in a kiss curl. And he'd never wanted anyone so badly than he wanted her right at that moment. He quite literally ached with the need to punish and possess. To take her so thoroughly that he would wipe any other man from her consciousness.

Alicia opened her eyes with effort. She had to stop this, had to make him see that this wasn't what he wanted. Not like this. She wanted to apologise for hitting him and, more than that, she realized that she wanted to explain…tell him the truth about what had really happened with Raul Carro.

But in a fast, efficient movement Dante had lifted her up into his arms and was striding to the bed. Alicia was still disorientated from the kiss, held against his chest as if she weighed no more than a bag of sugar.

'Wait,' she said weakly. 'Dante, we can't, really. I don't want this. Not like this.'

He stopped in his tracks and looked down into her eyes. Her pupils were so enlarged that her eyes looked black, mirroring his own. *She felt it too.*

'Don't lie,' he said tightly.

'I'm not lying…'

'You are. You want this so badly that, even now, even though you hate me, you want me. I know, *cara*, because it's the same for me.'

A cold feeling settled into her heart even as her betraying body's temperature seemed to soar under that look. He put her down on her feet and undid the tightly tied belt on her robe. Alicia stood still, her head downbent as he shucked it off her shoulders and down her arms. A sense of inevitability washed through her. What could she do? He was right, she'd be lying if she said she didn't want this too. This was the only pure communication they had, without words, their bodies didn't lie to each other. She hungered for him again so intensely that it washed away all other concerns.

He tipped up her chin with a finger and she forced herself to look blank, not to let him see the pain.

'Take off your clothes.' His demand made an erotic shiver skate down her spine. She felt sickened and angry with herself for even thinking of complying. But, with a shameful weakness that proved to be stronger than her will, her hands went to her buttons. A rogue part of her wanted to drive him to the edge of his control now. Without taking her eyes off his, she undid them one by one. The top slipped to the floor with the robe and then she pushed the trousers down and stepped out of them.

Dante looked down her body. Took in her small, high, pointed breasts, the tips puckering under his look. He'd had to ask her to undress because he wasn't sure that his hands wouldn't have shaken with everything that had just happened, with the desire that pumped through him, washing away all sanity and coherence, leaving only a need to take…and possess.

He took her hands and brought them to his shirt, instructing her with his eyes to undress him. Alicia's breath had long ago become laboured. Her fingers were clumsy on the buttons, the heat of his skin making her want to sag against him. Until finally somehow his shirt was free. His trousers were next. She pushed them down, taking his briefs with them, freeing that turgid, pulsing centre of his masculinity and desire. Her mouth went dry as she looked at him, wondering how she'd taken him before…

'Touch me.'

She looked up, feeling dazed and then slowly put out a hand

and encircled the hard shaft. It felt hot and silky with a steel core. Dante's jaw clenched, his eyes looked bright, glittering, the muscles in his neck corded and his chest swelled as she moved her hand up and down. Her naive skill made stars dance in front of his eyes and made him immediately correct what he'd thought—there was no naive about it, she was a witch.

He had to stop her, he'd had no idea her touch alone could send him so close to the edge. So he stopped her hand, for one brief moment his hand lay over hers and their eyes met. It was a moment so loaded with sexual tension that he nearly did explode. With supreme control called from somewhere, Dante moved their hands away and pressed her down on the bed.

Alicia was gone. She was in another place and, like the first time they'd made love, she welcomed it. As Dante stroked his hands down her body over silky skin, he lowered his mouth and suckled at her breasts, rousing the peaks to pink tips that looked angry they were so tightly aroused. She could feel the waves building; she was going to come even though he hadn't even entered her yet!

And then she felt him move down and he spread her legs with his big hands; they came under her buttocks, gripping tight and holding her open to his gaze and...mouth. She wanted to tell him to stop, wanted to say that this was *too* intimate, but her voice wouldn't work. Her head sagged back against the mattress as his lips, mouth and tongue sought and found and paid homage to her secret sensitive core. Her immediate instinct was to close her legs but Dante ruthlessly held them apart. She was laid open, bare...like some wanton. And she couldn't help herself as the tension spiralled out of control and her hips bucked unashamedly towards him as he held her and teased out every last ounce of pleasure from her quivering form.

Like the last time, just when she thought she couldn't possibly take any more, he moved up her body and lifted her on to the bed more fully. She looked up at him with big eyes. A fine sheen of sweat covered her body and Dante smoothed his hand over the curve of one breast.

'I can't…again, Dante, it's too much…' *Please!*

She couldn't deny it any more—the reason why she succumbed so readily. Her experience with Raul Carro hadn't come close to what this man made her feel with just a look, and that scared her witless. She was *literally* a naked quivering mass of vulnerability and this man was going to devastate her beyond anything she'd endured before.

'No, *cara.*' He bent his head to hers, taking her mouth, one hand possessively splayed across her breast, fingers trapping a nipple. He pulled back for a moment. 'We haven't even begun; when I leave this morning, you're never, ever going to forget this.'

Or me…

And, with ruthless and remorseless precision, he was true to his word; he entered her and took her soul soaring high above to a place she'd never been before—again and again. First he was slow and languorous, the second time was urgent, passion consuming them as he took her with an intensity that left her boneless. And the third time, in the shower, she wrapped her legs around his waist and cried out as he clenched his buttocks, driving up into her hard. She had to cling on to him as weak as a kitten afterwards, too afraid to stand because she knew she'd fall down.

Then he deposited her on the bed in an exhausted naked sprawl, calmly dressed and informed her that he'd see her for dinner that evening at seven.

When the door shut behind him, Alicia welcomed the fog of exhaustion, pulled the cover over her and sank into a mind-numbingly blank sleep.

CHAPTER FOURTEEN

IT WAS only when Dante had closed the door and was walking away that his composure faltered slightly. He remembered the shower, how she'd felt around him as he'd thrust into her again and again. How the little moans had become cries as her orgasm had broken at the same moment as his. The feeling of his flesh encased in hers... At that moment he'd not been able to imagine anyone else in the world driving him to such heights of pleasure.

And had she really pressed a kiss to his cheek and whispered brokenly into his ear, as he'd thrust deeply, that she was sorry for slapping him? He stared at himself in the mirror of the lift. He looked the same. But he didn't feel the same. He felt as if somehow a protective layer had been stripped from his epidermis. He touched his cheek where she had kissed him and knew it had happened, knew she'd said the words, but why?

And when she'd been unable to stand afterwards, she'd clung on to him so weakly that he'd had to carry her, and even as he'd laid her, exhausted, on the bed, his own body had been ready to take her again…and he couldn't help a dart of self recrimination—she was so small; he knew that very likely she'd be sore…

'You look pale, dear; are you all right?'

Alicia forced herself to smile and nodded at Patricia. She'd persuaded the other woman to meet her out on the decking overlooking the beach for aperitifs before dinner, leaving a note for Dante in the room. It was a pretty pathetic way of trying to prolong the inevitable—seeing him again. Humiliation still burned through her when she thought of the morning and how ruthlessly he'd made her his, he might as well have branded her with a cattle iron.

And when she thought of how she'd felt compelled to kiss his cheek and whisper, 'Sorry' in his ear, she cringed.

'Ah, here he is now.'

Alicia froze. She stood slowly. She was still sore, muscles aching all over and especially between her legs. She turned with extreme reluctance to face her nemesis and everything flew out of the window.

An emotion so strong rushed through her as she watched him walk towards her with that innate animalistic grace that she had to grip the chair back behind her. His dark eyes were unreadable and flickered down her body as he came close and leant in to kiss her on the lips. *Ever the act.* Pain skewered through her. His kiss was swift and hard and she couldn't avoid it. A blush stained her cheeks as a tingle started up between her legs, treacherously banishing the aches and tenderness.

Dante greeted Patricia too and engaged in banal conversation as he sat down and ordered a drink but he was supremely aware of Alicia. Her hair was down, around her shoulders in curly tendrils. She was dressed in a simple black jersey dress. With long sleeves it looked almost demure but for the deep V at the front, which showed tantalizing glimpses of her cleavage. His hand clenched around his glass; he didn't want anyone else looking at her, imagining sliding their hands under the material to cup and caress her breast.

Both women were looking at him expectantly, Alicia with an unmistakable wariness in her eyes. Again, he had the uncomfortable sensation that perhaps this morning he'd been too demanding…and yet she'd been so responsive, with him every step of the way, with those soft breathy moans.

'I'm sorry, I was miles away.' *With a witch…*

He shot her an irritated look and she blanched. And just then he saw the slightly bruised looking shadows under her eyes. An uneasy prickling assailed him for a second before he quashed it. He forced himself to concentrate on Patricia's chatter until Derek joined them.

As they walked out of the hotel and down the road to the restaurant they'd booked for dinner Dante took Alicia's hand and noticed something—on her feet were black flip-flops. She noticed him looking and grimaced. 'I'm sorry, I didn't think, if they won't let me in without…' She stopped. 'Look, I'll just run back and get proper shoes.'

He could see the red weals on the backs of her heels; they still looked sore and angry.

'No,' he said gruffly, vowing then that if anyone so much as looked at her strangely for wearing flip-flops that they'd go somewhere else. 'It's fine. They obviously need to heal.'

The relief on her face made him feel very strange, even as the unsavoury events of the day warred for supremacy in his chest. This woman was making a serious habit of turning his life upside down. And he was letting her.

'They should be better by tomorrow; I've been putting cream on them all day. It's my own fault; I'm not used to wearing those kind of shoes.'

He looked away from her huge brown eyes and hardened his heart. He cursed himself for the umpteenth time that day for letting her and her complications into his life. The woman was like a sledgehammer between his eyes; he couldn't see straight or think straight with her around.

* * *

In the restaurant, once they'd ordered, Alicia forced herself to relax and looked around. She caught Derek's eye and smiled but he blushed a little and then looked away guiltily. This was so far removed from the genial joky man she knew that she reached over without thinking. Dante and Patricia were deep in conversation beside them.

'Derek? What is it—is something wrong?'

He looked at her again and now looked unbelievably guilty *and worried*. The conversation stopped beside them and Alicia caught Patricia nudging Derek, as if to tell him to behave. Now she looked guilty too when she caught Alicia's look. Alicia felt sick to her stomach.

'What is it? Please.'

Even Dante beside her couldn't distract her from this.

Eventually he was the one who bit out, 'You may as well tell her; we already spoke about it this morning.'

Her insides froze. And she beseeched Patricia with her eyes.

With extreme reluctance and a very apologetic smile, she spoke. 'Alicia, dear, I'm afraid there's a very nasty rumour going around…about you.'

Her chest felt tight and hard. 'Let me guess. Serena Gore-Black.'

Patricia nodded. 'I'm so sorry. It's nobody's business what your history is, but there is the fear that the paparazzi will get a hold of the story. Gossip will always flourish where money, power and the media are prevalent…' Her voice trailed away and now Alicia felt doubly sick.

'My goodness, I never thought—'

'That your misdeeds would catch up with you?' Dante asked harshly.

Patricia jumped to her defence. 'Dante, that's no way to talk—'

Alicia put out a shaky hand, her head pounding with the implications of this hitting her like a truck. 'Patricia, please. The truth is…the truth is…it is true.'

Alicia knew she couldn't act the martyr—didn't want to. Dante would believe the worst of her in connection with Melanie until that baby was born, but *this*...she could try and do something about.

'In *one* way,' she said, her voice strong.

Everyone looked at her and she decided to focus on Patricia, her ally.

'The truth is yes, I did have an affair with a married man, Dr Raul Carro. But the other side of it—' her voice became bitter '—is that I had no idea he was married.'

She felt Dante go still beside her and couldn't bear to look and see blatant disbelief on his face. She continued, faltering. 'He came over for just a couple of months from Spain. No wedding ring, no mention of a wife and family...'

She shrugged minutely, bitterly aware of the glaring parallels between that situation and now this one when she said, 'He was tall, dark and handsome. In grim and grey January, in a bleak part of Oxford, he seemed like some kind of god, and when he asked me out...'

'You couldn't resist...' Patricia smiled with innate feminine understanding and she reached for Alicia's hand. 'Oh, my dear, you must have been devastated when you found out.'

Alicia sent a quick glance to Dante but he was staring into his drink.

'It was pretty horrendous.' She forced a hard smile. 'Especially when it turned out that he'd been seeing not only me, but half of the hospital staff, it seemed. I only found out at the very end. Serena Cox, as she was then, was one of his casualties and the first one to find out he was married. She made the phone call to his wife...but was very careful to absolve herself of any crime. She always denied her affair with him.'

Alicia felt icy-cold. It became actually potentially even worse. She continued faintly, avoiding Dante's eyes, 'Serena even leaked the story to a local rag and named people in an effort to deflect attention from herself.'

Alicia didn't have to remind herself that she had been one of those most prominently named and shamed. 'It didn't make the nationals…but…' In her mind's eye she could still see the lurid headline:

Dirty Doc does it with half the hospital while poor wifey waits at home…

Dante muttered caustically, 'This just gets better and better.'

For the first time, Alicia thought of how this would affect Derek too, with the welfare of his own company hinging on this merger, and had an image of their four children. She felt as if she were going to vomit.

Derek's voice boomed and he gasped with comic affront, 'And now that cow is trying to make you look bad!'

Alicia shrugged, barely keeping her panic contained. She could feel an icy wind coming from Dante's direction—no doubt he didn't believe a word of this. 'We'd never got on working together; it was obviously too good an opportunity for her to miss.'

Derek mopped his sweaty brow with a napkin and said forcibly, 'I don't have a problem with Gore-Black; he's a good man, just married to an unfortunate wife. She'll have to go home, of course. We do not need people here who want to distract and disrupt proceedings with foul play, do we, Dante?'

Dante looked at Alicia and his eyes were hard. She barely registered Derek's words. After a long moment he said, 'No. No, we don't.'

He was obviously regretting his decision to bring her after all and, as much as she would have welcomed a scenario which would have given her an out, Alicia was sickened to be the cause of creating a scandal within the negotiations—the very kind of scandal that could cause their collapse.

Later, as they said goodnight to the other couple, Patricia said, 'Alicia, don't worry, Derek is so angry that I wouldn't be surprised if that woman will be on a plane home tomorrow.'

Alicia grasped her hand, her face going pale. 'Oh, no, please; that'll just made things ten times worse.'

But Patricia just patted her cheek and said goodnight, telling her not to worry.

Later, when Alicia emerged into the bedroom after having a bath, the room was empty. Wrapping the towel tight around herself, she walked to the glass doors and found Dante sitting on the balcony, a glass of wine in his hand. He looked so cold and remote that she felt scared.

Did he think she'd made it all up? She couldn't bear for him to think that. She came out hesitantly. 'Dante…'

His head came up and his look sliced through her, telling her exactly what he thought of her. This was the lowest point she'd hit. She knew that.

'Go to bed, Alicia. I'm not in the mood for any more lies and revelations.'

Mute and stung and heartsore, Alicia turned around and went back inside. She curled up into a tight ball and only fell asleep when she heard Dante come in a long time later. He got in beside her but made no move to pull her close or make love to her.

Feigning sleep the following morning, Alicia only got up when she was sure Dante had gone. She got dressed and paced the room. She hated this—not only was her own private humiliation now public knowledge but it was putting Dante in a very awkward position.

She would have to go. Leave. That was it, there was no other recourse. She couldn't stay and give that vindictive cow, Serena Gore-Black, a reason to undermine Dante and Derek. She couldn't feel angry; even she could see how her story might look. Derek and Patricia were lovely people who had had no reason to mistrust her on sight, as Dante had, so of course they would give her the benefit of the doubt. And she loved them for that.

Ignoring the ache in her heart—in every limb—she packed her bag and then thought, what was the point? She didn't even own these clothes anyway. She dressed in the shabbiest clothes she could find, which, of course, were a pair of exquisite linen trousers and a beautiful white shirt. She dug out her phone and her credit card. She should have enough to get her home, with any luck.

She sat down and wrote a note to Dante, telling him that she was sorry she'd caused his own reputation to come into disrepute when he'd needed to be so careful about appearances. She wished him luck with the rest of the meetings, saying that she hoped that there wouldn't be any adverse effects. She didn't have any doubt that he'd be only too happy to see the back of her, after seeing the way he'd looked at her last night, when he believed she'd lied…she shivered.

Alicia used the last of her cash getting to the airport. She'd managed to evade the ever present paparazzi outside the hotel by getting a lift with one of the hotel workers from the back entrance to the main road in town. When she finally got to the ticket desk to ask for a one way fare to the UK, she could have wept with relief when the card was accepted. It was surely maxed to the hilt by now.

She made her way, following a long queue to the security desks and boarding gates. She caught a flurry of movement out of the corner of her eye and looked around. Her mouth dropped open when she saw Serena and her husband Jeremy with a mountain of luggage and about three people helping them. Her husband looked very red in the face and Serena was sulky, and then she looked over and saw Alicia.

Alicia had to blink. Surely she was seeing things? But no, Serena was stalking over in her high heels, venom in her blue eyes, spittle coming out of her mouth as she shrieked at Alicia, 'Are you happy now? Now that everyone knows that I was duped as well?' She flung a hand back to her embarrassed looking husband. 'I've been sent packing like a naughty child—'

And like something from a cartoon, suddenly Serena was gone, moved bodily out of the way, and Dante stood in front of her. She looked up and up. The queue was now snaking around Alicia, people looking at her and the little drama avidly.

He arched a brow. 'Going somewhere?'

'Home,' she said faintly. Someone jostled her and Dante took her arm and, picking up her bag, he walked her away from the line of people. She stopped in her tracks. 'Hang on a second. What are you doing here? Didn't you get my note?'

'I got your note and threw it out.'

'But why? I'm going home.' She crossed her arms and looked at him mutinously. 'I'm not going back there to be the cause of your embarrassment.'

'Don't you get it?' he asked, as if talking to a small child.

She shook her head.

'Serena is going home.'

'But that's just going to make things worse,' she wailed, her arms going down by her sides. 'What's to stop her going to the press at home?'

Dante shook his head, the light in his eyes making her breath stop. 'She won't be doing anything of the sort. Her husband is so mortified that he's threatened to cut her off and divorce her if she so much as breathes a further word of this. Derek went to them this morning. Of course her husband knew the full *real* story; she would have had to defend herself to him in case he ever found out about it. It didn't take much to get her to make a confession that she had maliciously twisted the truth to make you look bad. She deliberately caused the rumour but luckily it hasn't reached Buchanen's ears.'

Alicia's mouth dropped open again, her eyes wide. 'But how on earth…?'

Dante shrugged. 'It doesn't matter now. I owe you an apology. I'm sorry for doubting you, Alicia.'

She just looked at him. The way he was looking at her now was making her blood melt and flow like molten liquid.

He held out a hand. 'So please, will you come back with me?'

Alicia looked at his hand and then back at the queue snaking behind her. She knew if she'd ever had a chance of leaving, this was it. She looked at him briefly. 'I know I agreed to come and be…with you for the conference…but…' Her mind seized up, the awful reality was that she couldn't even contemplate walking away.

Dante could see the struggle on her face, in her eyes. If she turned and walked away now… But at that moment he felt her small hand creep into his palm and he closed his tight around it, relief shocking him as it surged through him. Before she could change her mind, he pulled her outside and into the car.

CHAPTER FIFTEEN

AS HE drove back into the city Alicia tried to take in everything that had just happened. She could feel him looking at her.

'When you said Raul Carro had been the cause of you going to Africa…you meant to get away from him?'

Alicia nodded. 'It was so horrific. His poor wife…I still feel awful about it. I always will.'

'But you didn't know.'

'It doesn't matter; it feels even worse, he was such an operator. In a way, I'm actually glad Serena called his wife. She had to know, and he had to be found out.'

'But he *was* in Africa?'

'Yes, but not till the end. He came just days before I left.' Disgust made her voice tight. 'He barely recognized me and I could see already that he was making the move on various nurses…'

'Do you still love him?' Dante didn't know why he'd asked the question or why his hands tightened on the steering wheel as he waited for Alicia's answer. He glanced at her but she was looking straight ahead; she seemed to be locked in another place. He wanted to reach out and turn her face to him so that he could see her eyes—and read what? he asked himself angrily.

After a long moment she said, 'No. And I don't think I ever did, to be honest.' *Not now that I know what real love feels like…and it's a million times more scary…* Alicia felt as though she stood on moving tectonic plates—one false move and she'd disappear down into a crack for ever.

Dante's hands tensed on the wheel again as another wave of relief flowed through him. When he'd found her gone and the note in the room, his insides had seized with panic. At the thought that she could just disappear like that, out of his life, gone. It had made him feel out of control… And that was before Derek had found him and told him what he'd found out. Which had made him feel even more out of control.

He flicked the woman beside him a glance. She was still here. And, he told himself, that was all that mattered because he needed her to maintain this precious respectability, which was now restored. *When you've never let it bother you before?* He shut out the voice and concentrated on the traffic.

That night they sat out on the balcony of their suite and shared an after dinner liqueur. Alicia felt very much as if they'd turned a corner, but to go where? Dante had apologized for judging her wrongly but she couldn't really blame him in the first place as she hadn't defended herself, not seeing the point. And, now that she had stayed, she felt as if her heart were visibly beating on her sleeve, plain for all to see.

'What are you thinking about?'

Alicia blushed and choked slightly on her drink. She could just imagine the look on his face if she told him. Instead she shrugged. 'Nothing in particular.' She felt him turn more fully towards her and found herself tensing slightly.

'Did you go to Africa to punish yourself?'

She jerked her head to look at him, eyes widening. 'What on earth do you mean?'

His face was dark, unreadable and she felt naked, extremely vulnerable.

'I was just wondering if part of your motivation for going there was in some way a reaction to what had happened.'

Alicia looked away from him again, out to the inky, starry darkness. Her mind whirled. She'd never thought of it like that, but *had* she chosen to go there as some sort of penance? At times, it certainly had felt like a punishment of sorts. She could feel him looking at her intently and desperately wanted his penetrating mind and gaze off her.

She shrugged slightly. 'It certainly played a part in my reasons for going…but I hadn't thought about it too much, to be honest.' *And for him to be the one to assess the psychology behind her reasons?* Again, her head swirled and she felt unbelievably vulnerable. She took more than a sip from her drink and then turned to him, seizing on the first thing that came to mind to take his attention from her.

'Will you tell me something about yourself…? It just feels a little funny…not really knowing anything about you.' She'd been about to add on, *After all, you're going to be my niece or nephew's uncle,* but stopped herself in time, not wanting to open that can of worms.

He looked at her darkly. 'What do you want to know?'

She shrugged, relieved that they'd moved off the subject of her. 'I don't know… How did you get to where you are now if you came from the streets…and what about your parents…?'

She held her breath. He looked away from her and she could see his jaw clench. When he spoke it was flat and emotionless, it made something go cold inside Alicia, because she recognized that it hid huge pain.

'When my brother was one and I was six, my mother left us. My father had taken off long before that to God knows where, and Paolo's father was another wastrel. We were taken into an orphanage but it closed down a few years later due to lack of funds. So we lived on the streets and carved a niche for ourselves there.'

'You and your brother?'

He nodded.

'How old were you then?'

'Thirteen, fourteen.'

He was silent for so long then that Alicia thought he'd had enough and she opened her mouth to speak but then he said, 'One day a man saw me doing some labour, helping to build a house. He called me over and offered me a job there and then.' He glanced at her briefly. 'I said I could only take it if I could bring my brother with me.'

'But Paolo…'

'Paolo was about nine then and running around getting into trouble.'

'This man, Stefano Arrigi, took us in. He mentored me.' He shrugged. 'Said he saw something in me that he'd never seen in anyone else, and I worked hard. He had no family. When he died I was twenty-one and he left his small construction business to me.'

'And now the business is known all over the world…'

He nodded again with no apparent pride. Just quiet modesty.

Alicia's heart ached for the young man he'd been… She understood because she too had suffered a similar fate, albeit not ending up on the streets, thank goodness. But somehow she knew that he wouldn't appreciate her baring her soul, and she still felt far too vulnerable to reveal any more about herself. But it gave her an insight into his complex character and when he stood to lead her inside, clearly done with talking, she knew that, despite her best efforts, she had just fallen even harder in love with him.

When they returned to their suite the following Sunday evening from a group wine tasting trip to the beautifully leafy area of

Stellenbosch, Alicia picked up a piece of paper that gave the details of a medical unit that was going to be in the hotel for the rest of the conference. She looked at him warily. 'What's this about?'

Dante stood apart from her, arms folded. 'While I thought you were off sightseeing all last week, I found out from Patricia that you were acting as an impromptu Florence Nightingale…'

He seemed almost angry. And Alicia had no idea why. It seemed like, no matter what she did, she'd end up annoying him somehow. They'd shared a comparative truce for the rest of the week but all weekend he'd been dark and brooding.

'You don't have to go to the expense of this. I don't mind looking after the odd child with sunburn or someone with a tummy upset—'

He lifted a hand and ticked off fingers. 'Or a child with a sprained ankle, or a man who can't sleep, or the receptionist with cramps, or—'

'OK, OK, stop.' She held up her hands, aghast that he knew this. 'If I'd known you'd mind so much I wouldn't have offered to help.'

Dante's head whirled with the way the whole anatomy of this relationship—this *situation,* he corrected angrily—had changed utterly. Alicia had endeared herself not only to his close friends, the O'Briens, but to everyone else too, it seemed. Buchanen's wife, who had arrived towards the end of last week, was in raptures over the fact that she and Alicia shared the vocation of nursing. He couldn't move for people stopping him and telling him how great she was, how sweet she was, how kind she was…

And it was killing him. Because he knew what she was. The facts were stark. Until that baby was born, the jury was out on Alicia and Melanie Parker. And he would be the biggest prize fool to forget it. Because he knew he was in danger of succumbing, believing in the myth. He'd seen the myth before and it had revealed a very ugly truth. This was when he had to be most vigilant.

He could cope with the fact that Alicia was what she was because he was equipped to deal with a woman like her. But he was angry with her dogged persistence in maintaining this… façade. He forced himself to cool down. Years before, it had affected him, but not any more. *He was in control now.* No matter what happened. All he was interested in was sating his physical hunger, which burned through him like a bushfire.

He strolled towards her and tipped her chin up. 'Oh, I don't mind, Alicia. I just don't like sharing you around…that's all.'

His possessiveness should have excited her but it didn't, because the dark coldness in his eyes hinted at an emotion that began and ended with physical desire. He didn't want her to stop because he *cared* about her…foolish girl.

Tears pricked the back of her eyes as he claimed her mouth and the familiar sensations washed through her body. Nothing had changed. He still didn't trust her, he still thought that she and Melanie had concocted some plan to extort money…and after the end of next week she would be gone, back home.

CHAPTER SIXTEEN

'I WANT you to come back to Italy and stay with me in Rome.'

Alicia felt dizzy when Dante said the words. They were so far removed from what she would have expected to hear.

And lying on her back, naked, with Dante propped up on one arm beside her, also naked and visibly aroused, was not the best place to be when he said that.

It was the end of the second week. The following evening they were due to fly back to Europe from Cape Town. The negotiations were over and they had been a great success. Buchanen had signed the contracts in a big press conference along with Derek and Dante just yesterday. Work was due to start on the sports stadium within the next year.

That morning they'd travelled down to a luxurious hideaway hotel in a small town called Arniston Bay on the stunningly picturesque Garden Route. Alicia hadn't questioned Dante's impetuous decision, made when one of the South African staff in the hotel had offered to fly them down there on the tiny private hotel jet.

She'd grabbed at the chance to be alone with him. And all day Alicia had existed in a haze of self-deluded, fuzzy fantasy. She and Dante had explored the white, white sands and rolling dunes and had swum in the dark blue sea.

And now he was asking her to stay on, to come back and keep indulging in the dream? Her head said, *That way lies madness and pain,* but her heart just said, *Go.*

'But…' she struggled to try and make sense of what he was saying '…why would you want that?'

'Because what we have is good…' Here he ran a hand up over her belly to cup her breast.

Immediately it tightened and her breathing changed. She pulled his hand down. 'But—'

'I'm not ready to let you go,' he cut in arrogantly and placed his hand back on her breast, his fingers trapping her nipple now and making her eyes close as she bit back a moan. She trapped his hand with hers, but that just made it feel even more erotic, with her hand on his over her breast. She took it away again quickly.

'Dante, I'm not some kind of pet… You can't *keep* me.'

'And can you really tell me that you're ready to leave, to walk away from *this…*?'

He moved on to his back and pulled her up over him in one fluid movement so that she straddled him. He spread her legs around him with his big hands. She could feel his erection and bit her lip.

No, she wasn't ready to leave him… She loved him, like a fool.

Abruptly he moved again, sitting up and, taking Alicia with him, he lifted her slightly before lowering her back down on to his rigid shaft. She gasped and wrapped her arms around his neck. Her breasts were crushed against him, her legs wrapped tight around his waist, ankles locked behind him and as he moved and surged within her she looked deep into his eyes as they both crested the wave. It was this intense, this amazing, every single time. And he was right—she couldn't walk away.

Breathing jaggedly in the aftermath, sweat on her brow, her limbs shaking, Dante pressed a kiss to her damp neck and asked again, 'So…what's it to be?'

Two Months Later…

A smile of pure masculine satisfaction curved Dante's mouth as he walked into his apartment in the centre of Rome. He could hear the shower running and was already imagining Alicia, twisting and turning under the spray, hair in long tendrils down her back.

He shed his clothes with indecent haste and his smile got bigger as he walked confidently to the door of the bathroom. His desire was as strong as ever, if not even more urgent. He opened the door and saw the small figure through the steam, hands held high washing her hair, lifting her breasts. He stepped in and she jumped in fright.

'Dante!'

'*Si…cara.* Here, let me do that…'

She let him turn her so that he could run his hands around her front to cup her soapy breasts. He smiled again against her skin and when he pressed close, letting her feel his erection and a shudder ran through her, he knew that he'd made the right decision in making Alicia his mistress. Life was good.

Later, Alicia looked at Dante across the dinner table in the apartment. With each day that went by she was falling deeper and deeper into a dark hole that threatened to engulf her utterly. For the past two months she'd been playing a role—the role of his mistress. A fool's role. Perfectly compliant, by his side for every occasion and always a smile on her face hiding the fact that, inside, she didn't even know how her heart kept on beating.

He was as astoundingly gorgeous as ever. Even more so. He'd let his hair grow a little, which had softened his features. She sighed and played with her wineglass, having to take her eyes away because it simply hurt to look at him.

He reached across and took her hand, turning it palm up. She steeled herself and looked at him as blandly as she could. 'There's a function on this Sunday night for my charity in Milan…and on Saturday we have the annual Lake Como water sports competition for the kids… You will come?'

As if she had a choice… She could have laughed. What might she say? Actually, no, I want to stay here in Rome in this cool and sterile apartment, alone…

She forced a smile. 'Of course, that would be lovely.'

He smiled too and it made her chest tight. No words of affection, no words of tenderness or love. And Alicia wouldn't be able to hold out for much longer, because she knew that the only reason she'd come at all, had even agreed to this arrangement, was because she had stupidly dreamt that perhaps, with a bit of time to get to know each other, Dante would come to feel *something* for her. Instead, she'd come to realize that he felt nothing for anybody. His brother, maybe. But that was it.

The awful thing was, she couldn't fault him. He was attentive, considerate, generous to a fault…and, as for the bedroom… When he'd surprised her in the shower earlier, it had scared her how much her body still craved his…needed his. Even after this period of time. No, she thought firmly to herself, she would have to be strong, would have to walk away…soon…as soon as she had the strength.

That Saturday, Dante drove them in a Jeep to the part of the lake which was the water sports centre. They'd arrived at the villa last night from Milan and Alicia had been delighted to see Julieta again, and even had a few words of Italian to try out this time—she'd been taking classes in Rome. The weather was unusually warm for October. In jeans and a T-shirt with a light fleece top, Alicia was relieved to have been able to get some clothes more suited to her own naturally casual style.

When they arrived about a hundred children ranging from three years old to seventeen, stood milling around near the pontoons. And as soon as they saw the Jeep a huge cheer went up. Alicia couldn't believe it when Dante stopped and got out; they all rushed forward to greet him, some of the younger ones already tugging at his hands and pulling him forwards. She was so stunned that she nearly fell out of the jeep. He looked back at her and smiled ruefully before he was swallowed in the crush. Alicia had never seen him look so boyish…or *happy*.

A young woman with a pleasant smile approached her. 'You must be Alicia.'

She nodded and smiled.

'I'm Maria, the manager of the orphanage.' She gestured to the kids. 'They've been so excited for weeks now; this trip is one of the most popular every year.'

'You mean there are others?'

Maria nodded. 'Oh, yes, we have several, here and in Milano—all over Italy, actually. Water sports, activity centres, horse-riding…you name it.'

Alicia just shook her head, thoroughly bemused now to see Dante and several other instructors in wetsuits striding around and organizing the kids.

'Come on, I'll show you where you can sit and watch.'

Alicia followed Maria to a seating area that had a set of bleachers and they sat down. She explained to Alicia that the young adults were all ex-members of the orphanage and street centre who took time to come back and help out.

Alicia couldn't stop the ache in her heart. Here was the evidence—she watched as Dante caught a small girl up and held her high, making her laugh—he *could* love. He did have the capacity. Just not for her. And then she felt awful for even thinking of herself like that when these kids had no one…especially as she had been one. She *knew*.

She turned to Maria, pushing down the ache. 'OK, what can I do to help?'

Maria looked at her, clearly taken aback. 'You…you want to help?'

'Of course.' Alicia stood up. 'Come on, they all look like they're having way too much fun without us.'

That evening, as the sun set and the kids were changing out of their wetsuits, chattering and jumping around, Dante leant against a wall and took a deep slug from a bottle of beer. His eyes darted around and finally found what—*who*—he was looking for. And when he did, he wished he hadn't. She was still in a wetsuit, her hair a mass of damp curls on top of her head. She looked about eighteen and she had a queue of children lined up in front of her as she tended to each one, doling out plasters, rubbing cream into cuts and bruises. None of the children were really hurt beyond a couple of flesh wounds from horseplay but he'd never seen them line up like that before. His eyes went back to her. She hugged a little girl tight and kissed her on the head before sending her away with an affectionate pat on the bottom.

Maria came up beside him, shaking her head in awe, and said in Italian, 'Dante, she's—'

He cut her off ruthlessly. 'I know.' He took another sip of his beer. He didn't want to hear it. Since they'd come back to Italy, since he'd had Alicia more or less to himself apart from the odd social occasion, he'd convinced himself that he'd been in the first flush of some crazy lust phase in South Africa, letting her get to him like that, under his skin.

Keeping her in his apartment, exclusively for him, all he'd had to think about was sating the physical desire. They'd talked, yes, and he'd been pleased to discover that they had many common interests, her dry sense of humour that was so like his own…but it had only enhanced what was, for him, a very physical affair.

A short time later Alicia joined him at the Jeep, back in her own clothes. The kids had just been loaded back on to the bus— there had been too many for the plane—and it had pulled away with much beeping and shouting. She couldn't stop smiling.

'That was the best day…thank you. I really love—' She halted under his stern gaze, the words dying.

He frowned. 'What is it?'

She shook her head and he shrugged and went to her door, opening it. Her heart hammered. The words had been trembling on her lips, she'd been about to say, *love you*. And thank goodness she hadn't.

She walked to her door and he helped her in. She watched him walk around the front of the car and thought that she'd never figure him out, even if she had a lifetime.

That night, back at the villa, they made love with an almost savage intensity. It felt, inexplicably, as if they were heading for some kind of reckoning. As she lay in his arms afterwards, unable to sleep but listening to his breathing even out and deepen, Alicia knew that intensity had come from her because the time had come to walk away. Today she'd felt something close to normal again—interacting with the children, tending to them, had been so rewarding. She knew that with each day that passed she was diminishing more and more and soon she'd be a shadow of her former self.

'I'll be back this evening at six, the function starts at half past, and Signora Pasquale will deliver the dress at five.'

'Dante, there's no need for a new dress—it's crazy—I've brought some with me.'

He shook his head. 'I told you before, the cost is nothing. And tonight is important.'

Alicia shrugged and watched him get up from the lunch table.

They were back in his palazzo in Milan, in preparation for the big charity ball. They'd arrived by helicopter earlier that morning. Patrizia was gone, back to school, and her mother was in residence again.

When he had gone, Alicia wandered around a little disconsolately. She tried to phone Melanie to see how she was but there was no answer at the house in London. And she couldn't get through on either her mobile or Paolo's. She wasn't unduly worried, she knew they usually went for a gentle stroll in the late afternoon if Paolo could get off work early.

Signora Pasquale's assistant arriving distracted her and by the time she'd washed and dressed, it was nearly six.

Alicia heard his steps on the stairs but stayed looking out of the window. He approached behind her, his scent winding around her like a sensual cloak. And, like clockwork, her heart started to thud heavily, her pulse jumped. He came very close then and pressed a kiss to the bare back of her neck, she closed her eyes in response and at the sweet pain that gripped her.

'*Bella,* Alicia.'

She turned around then and he swept that hot black gaze up and down, taking in gold chiffon folds that fell from under her bust in layers, down to her feet.

His brow quirked. 'Shoes?'

She stuck out a foot and showed him the funky gold wedges Signora Pasquale had found. She smiled even as her heart ached. 'I've learnt my lesson one too many times now. Me and heels just do not go. Wedges are the way forward.'

Her hair was piled high, curly tendrils escaping. Golden hoop earrings swung against her slim neck, a single gold bangle encircled her tiny wrist.

Dante's chest felt tight. 'Let's go.'

Despite the wedges, Alicia's feet were beginning to hurt. The dinner was long over but people still milled around the glittering ballroom in one of Milan's oldest buildings. Dante had given a speech, again showing her, uncomfortably, that if he had a passion for something, he was a force to be reckoned with. She took a sip of champagne, she wasn't going to wallow in *that* self-pity again.

And then he was striding towards her through the crowd. He came and took the glass from her and lifted her hand to his mouth, kissing her in full view of everyone. Something in

Alicia's chest hardened—still the act, the show of public respectability. He was certainly getting his money's worth, she thought with uncharacteristic cynicism.

They started to make their way out of the room and were almost at the door when Dante stopped so rapidly that Alicia bumped into his back. She looked around to see what the hold up was and saw a woman addressing him. She looked to be a few years senior to Alicia, closer to Dante's age. And she was very beautiful. Thick black hair, dark olive skin and green almond eyes… In fact, she was exquisite. More than exquisite.

Alicia couldn't understand what they were saying but she didn't mistake Dante's tension or the way his hand had tightened almost painfully on hers. He'd even moved her so that she was a little behind him, as if to stop her witnessing this. Feeling suddenly enraged at this behaviour and even more so if this was some ex-lover of his, she pulled free and stepped around to face the woman.

Her green eyes were hard and cold and took Alicia aback. But she was determined to be the one to show good manners, even though her heart was breaking a little apart because surely this woman must have been a lover—she was too gorgeous not to have been.

She held out a hand. 'Hello, I'm Alicia.'

The woman just cast a disdainful look at her hand and turned back to Dante, a sneer on her lovely face—which didn't actually look so lovely any more. She spoke again, rapidly.

Dante said something harsh and the woman stopped talking, her mouth mutinous, ugly.

Alicia couldn't stop herself. 'Dante…who is this, please?'

He didn't even look at her; he kept looking at the woman, his expression so cold that it scared Alicia. 'This,' he said and his voice matched his look, 'is *no one.*'

And with that he grabbed her hand again and pulled her after him and out of the room.

CHAPTER SEVENTEEN

WHAT shook Alicia up more than anything was the thought that perhaps some day she'd run into him again, exactly like that, and he would look at her with the same arctic coldness while clutching the hand of another woman. And she couldn't bear it. She knew the moment had come and she almost welcomed the events of the evening, what she'd witnessed. It was a sign.

Once inside the dimly lit palazzo she pulled back from him when he would have reached for her hand to lead her up to bed.

He looked back at her, the impatience on his face nearly funny, except Alicia didn't feel like laughing. She spoke and thankfully her voice was steady. 'Dante, who was that woman?'

He frowned. 'It doesn't matter who she is; I told you she's no one.'

Again that chilling tone. It cut through her.

'Of course she's not no one Dante, she's a human being. An ex-lover?'

She held her breath.

'Why do you want to know?' he hurled out, getting angry. His reaction made her even more determined.

'I want to know, Dante, because whether you like it or not, we have a relationship and quite frankly it scared me the way you treated her.' She turned away from him, afraid he might see something in her eyes, and went into the drawing room. One lamp glowed in the corner, sending long shadows across the floor. She heard him come in behind her and turned back again, wrapping her arms around herself.

He stood in the doorway, six feet four inches of bristling, angry, taut *male*. And she had no idea why he was so angry.

'Well? Why can't you tell me? Is it a bit inconvenient having your lovers run into each other?' She laughed harshly. 'I'm surprised you're not used to it; after all there must be enough of us.'

He strode in and stopped just inches away; she could see that he was restraining himself from touching her. She wasn't scared; she knew he wouldn't touch her in violence. But he was livid.

'And which rag did you read that in, Alicia?'

'No, let's not make this about me. Your reputation is well-known, Dante; you said it yourself when you *asked* me so nicely to come to the conference in the first place.' A poisonous image inserted itself into her mind's eye, and the memory of the way he'd dismissed that other woman in his life so summarily. She couldn't stop, the words came pouring out. 'The woman on the steps of the hotel that night in Lake Como; you'd just come from her bed, hadn't you?'

A dull flush coloured his cheekbones. That memory was utterly toxic to him now.

'See? So please, spare me.' She folded her arms and moved back, chin tilted up with all the defiance she could muster. 'So are you going to tell me, or just run around the city bumping into women and freezing them out…the same way you'll freeze me out some day, no doubt.'

Dante couldn't believe they were having this conversation.

They should be in bed now. When he thought of that woman all he felt was disgust. And now Alicia was digging, insisting on finding out.

He felt stupid then, foolish. His first instinct when faced with Sonia had been to protect Alicia from her venomous presence; he'd even moved her behind him. And yet…the two women were peas in a pod. A hard, heavy, dense mass weighed his chest down. Talk about a sign to wake him up, having Alicia and Sonia come face to face like that.

He laughed harshly then. 'You want to know who she is?' *Because she is you and you are she; that's why you're so interested isn't it?*

He paced back and forth on the carpet like a caged panther and Alicia instinctively stepped away a little. His energy was lashing out like the end of a live wire.

'I'll tell you exactly who she is; you'll probably admire her. Her name is Sonia Paparo.' His mouth twisted with extreme distaste. 'And yes, we were lovers. A long time ago, when I inherited the business from Stefano. Actually, to be exact, the day after I made my first million she turned up on my doorstep. She had some lame story but I didn't care because she was the most beautiful thing I had ever seen in my life.'

Alicia backed away even further, every word a dart that cut and stung. But she had asked for it and knew he wouldn't stop now.

His accent was thicker. 'I told her all about myself because, well, when you're in love you do, don't you?' He didn't wait for an answer; his eyes were like burning coals.

'I told her how our mother left us, how angry I was, how hurt. How Paolo had pined for her for years, that he still pined for her. Then one day she arrived and had a woman with her, an old woman who knelt down at my feet and begged forgiveness for leaving me and Paolo.'

Alicia's hand went to her chest. Hearing the words was like watching a car crash in slow motion.

'I saw no reason not to believe Sonia's fantastic story of how she'd overheard this woman in the market talking about the two boys she'd deserted, and how much she regretted it. How she'd put two and two together. After all, why would she lie to me? She loved me. And I did look at it logically; it wasn't so unbelievably fantastical, we were still in the same area of Naples. The woman would have been around the right age, the same colouring…and she knew things about us…but it was only afterwards I realized that they were things I had told Sonia, together with a bit of intuition, supposition and women's innate deviousness thrown in for good measure.'

'Dante—' She put out a hand but he cut her off curtly.

'I'm not finished. So, against my best instincts, I welcomed the woman into my house. Too much had happened for me to forgive so quickly, but Paolo, being at an impressionable age, was ecstatic to have his mother back again, not that he'd even really known her in the first place. A huge part of me didn't believe…and Sonia accused me of being cynical, unbelieving. She pointed out how happy Paolo was…and I didn't want to be like that—cynical, mistrustful. I'd had a bellyful of it on the streets.'

Alicia felt a chair behind her and sat down dumbly. She watched as Dante still paced.

'I don't think I need to explain to you the importance of the mother in Italian families.' It wasn't a question and Dante had gone inwards to another place. Alicia could only sit and watch, mute.

'I knew Sonia expected a marriage proposal; she'd made it obvious from very early on. But I'd held back, I'd always vowed I'd never marry.' His mouth twisted in a parody of black humour. 'But, funnily enough, by then *Mama* was firmly ensconced in her new role and encouraging me daily to make an honest woman of Sonia. One day I came home to find them cackling together in the kitchen over how much money they would stand to get when I asked Sonia to marry me, as they predicted I was about to do any day.' He laughed harshly. 'And, more fool me, I'd even picked out a ring. Had stupidly listened to her advice.'

Alicia couldn't move.

He looked straight at her, through her, the pain in his eyes intense. 'Mother and daughter, con artists. It was a well worn ploy and we were the perfect victims. When I wasn't quick enough to propose, Sonia got creative. Between us, we wouldn't have really remembered our mother…but Paolo…I had to tell him the truth. He couldn't have borne the thought of being abandoned again.'

Alicia stood up and came over, her eyes anguished. 'Dante, I'm so sorry, truly…I know exactly how you must have felt—'

Her words cut into him, the wound still raw, and he couldn't believe how he'd been provoked into telling her about Sonia. He turned on her, eyebrows drawn together in fury. '*You?* How on earth could you ever know what it was like to be abandoned?'

He looked down his strong nose at her in disgust.

'I know,' she said quietly, 'because I watched my own mother walk away from me when I was four and Melanie was two and a half.'

Betrayal—all over again. The word resounded in his head, deafening him. For a minute there was silence and then the cold fury that blasted from Dante was worse than any hot temper.

'You…' He said something undoubtedly rude in Italian, his mouth a tight sneer. 'I tell you this and still you think that you can worm your way in with not only a baby but now a fairy tale of abandonment. You haven't even got the intelligence to try and make up a slightly better version, an even more lurid story to really tug on the heartstrings?'

Alicia was trying to make sense of this; she knew on some banal level that obviously he didn't believe her. And on another level this pain cut so deep that she didn't think she'd even make it from the room.

Dante looked at her, incandescent with rage at her blatant greed and audacity. Her eyes had closed with his words and now she looked dead ahead, through him. Her face was pale.

How could she do this? Didn't she see? Acting to the bitter end.

Yet, even in the midst of this he was aware of her, in a visceral way that eclipsed anything he'd felt for any other woman, even Sonia… It was the worst thing of all; it even made the naked greed and avarice seem unimportant… Something dark moved through him. And what it was, was this: he knew he couldn't let this woman go; he wasn't ready for that, no matter what. He assured himself he was still in control, even though he felt anything but.

'Nothing has changed, Alicia. We can get past this, at least we can be totally honest now.'

She lifted dead eyes to his and he took a step back. She laughed and it didn't sound like her. 'You just can't believe that your brother could fall in love with a girl—a nice girl, *a good girl*—have a baby and want to get married, can you? Because it didn't happen for you. You got tricked in a heinous way, Dante, but she was one woman and her very twisted mother…and I'm afraid, as inconveniently coincidental as it may sound, we do share a similar history of woe.'

She sounded incredibly weary all of a sudden. 'To be honest, I don't much care if you believe me, I should be used to it now, you haven't believed a word I've said since the moment we met and I've done nothing but tell the truth. And when I was wrong, I apologized. You can look up the records of the North London Orphanage Trust and you'll see our names there.'

'If this is true, then why didn't you tell me the night I told you about my past?'

She looked at him with a dull light dimming her eyes. 'Would you have listened, would you have believed me? It would have sounded just as fantastic then.'

Then she remembered something he'd said and her face paled even more with the hurt that sliced through her. 'And if you think that I could ever *admire* someone who could do something like that, then you don't know me at all.' She emitted a harsh sound somewhere between a laugh and a moan. It was a sound of pain, if Dante could only recognize it, but Alicia knew he wouldn't.

'Actually, do you know what, it's not even about knowing me, the truth is—you don't *want* to know me. All you want is a body in your bed.'

He took a step forward and opened his mouth to speak but just then his mobile rang shrilly in his pocket. With a grunt of irritation he plucked it out and answered it, his eyes never leaving Alicia's face. '*Si…*'

All she heard was rapid incomprehensible Italian, she turned away, wrapping her arms around herself and thinking of how she would try to get a flight tomorrow—get away. After hearing what Dante had been through, she could understand where his mistrust stemmed from. She knew now that that woman had taken his heart and crushed it to pieces before he'd had a chance to experience real love. She felt weary; she was obviously not the woman who could unlock his heart. There were too many awful similarities. It was cruel how the divine forces had brought them together.

'*Alicia.*'

She turned and opened her mouth, about to ask him to just let her go to bed—*without him*—and closed it again. His face looked bleak and had a completely different expression. Immediately adrenalin flowed through her.

'It's Melanie, isn't it? Something's wrong.'

He put out a hand to her shoulder and she flinched. He winced. 'Tell me.'

'She's been rushed into the clinic; they have to do an emergency Caesarean section.'

Her hand went to her chest. 'But she's only seven and a half months pregnant.'

She swayed and Dante put his arm around her, the abject fear and worry on her face mocking him and his obstinate suspicions. In that instant many things became clear to him and yet…so much was still obscured, but it would all have to wait now.

He helped her from the room, made her put on something more practical and within the hour they were taking off for England.

By the time they reached the clinic the early morning rush hour was starting to clog the autumnal London streets. Alicia didn't wait for her door to be opened; she ran from the car, straight inside. When she found the room, she burst in to find Melanie and Paolo holding hands, their faces wreathed in tired smiles.

She felt weak and had to cling to the door for support. Melanie was obviously exhausted but stretched out a hand, tears glistening in her eyes. 'Lissy, you're an aunt. You've got a beautiful baby niece called Lucia. She's tiny but strong, a little fighter. She's going to be fine.'

Alicia hugged Melanie so tight that she had to pull back for fear of hurting her. 'Oh, Mel, I've never been so worried in all my life…'

'We didn't bother calling because we knew you and Dante were on the way.'

Tears ran unchecked down her cheeks. Her sister seemed so different, so grown up…and so did Paolo, he looked like he'd become a man since she'd seen him last.

A shadow darkened the door. Dante. Alicia couldn't look. She barely heard Melanie telling Dante that he was an uncle, blissfully unaware of Dante's suspicious mind that would doubt the outcome until he had the results of the paternity test. The man had so many reasons to be mistrustful, but Alicia couldn't forgive him, not yet. Not when she knew he was going to put them through this final test.

She focused on Melanie and barely noticed Paolo leave the room to talk to his brother.

When Paolo came out into the corridor Dante was struck initially by how much more mature he seemed. Paolo stood in front of him, tall and proud and distant, and, for the first time, Dante regretted that he had been the one to put that distance there. Ever since his experience with Sonia he'd protected Paolo, dreading the day he too would be taken in. And he'd thought that, despite his best efforts, he had, but now…

'I'd like you to see something, Dante.'

He nodded and followed his brother down the corridor but then suddenly Paolo stopped in his tracks and looked at him.

'You don't even know how I met Melanie, do you?' Paolo answered himself with a sharp laugh. 'Of course not. You don't know that it wasn't even at work. We actually met at a fund-raiser for your charity…do you remember? Late last year when you were in South America for a few weeks and you asked me to be your envoy. She was there, Dante, because she does charity work in her spare time with a local orphanage that we subsidise. And do you know why?'

Dante could feel himself going pale, a sick feeling spreading outwards from his chest. He couldn't keep pretending to himself any more that it wasn't true.

But Paolo continued, oblivious. 'Because Melanie grew up in an orphanage too, Dante. With Alicia. Their mother left them, just like ours did.' His young mouth twisted and Dante hated to see the cynicism in his eyes. 'No doubt you don't believe that, though, probably think it's too convenient—'

'Paolo, stop.' His brother's words were too painfully reminiscent.

Paolo closed his mouth.

'I do. I do believe you. Alicia told me herself.' *I just didn't want to believe her…*

Paolo looked at him for a long moment and then kept walking until they got to a window. Just inside the glass were incubators and Paolo pointed to the nearest one. Dante saw a tiny olive-skinned baby with a head of thick dark hair. She wriggled and stretched and yawned, tiny hands opening and closing. And then he saw the name tag: Lucia D'Aquanni. The name of their mother.

He could feel a surge of such emotion rip upwards from his feet that he swayed and had to put a hand on the glass to steady himself. The only way he could deal with it and stay standing was to push it down. Deep.

Paolo faced him. 'Dante, you're my brother, I love you. I too went through what you did but it's not your job to keep protecting me.' His brother's eyes flashed. 'If you really want me to go ahead with the paternity test I will, but know this, it will only be for you and I will *never* look at it. I do not need proof that this is my baby. I *know,* and I love Melanie. We will be getting married. *No matter what.*'

Dante felt as if he were trying to climb up an incredibly steep and slippy slope. He put a heavy hand on Paolo's shoulder. 'I don't want you to do the test. And I'm sorry for ever asking you and putting you through this.'

His eyes asked his brother to forgive him and Paolo did, without question, straight away. Because he had been there too and he understood.

CHAPTER EIGHTEEN

ALICIA'S BACK TENSED when she sensed the brothers coming back into the room. She glanced up quickly and the bleak look on Dante's face made her blood run cold. She avoided Melanie's eye and looked at her hands.

Dante came to the end of the bed and Alicia could hear the breath he took. When he spoke his voice was clipped. 'Melanie, please accept my congratulations on your baby. You and Paolo have my best wishes and I am truly sorry for any hurt I may have caused.'

Alicia sensed his eyes settle on her for a moment, like a flash of sun passing through the parting clouds, but she kept looking resolutely down at her hands.

Her sister spoke with quiet dignity. Alicia saw Paolo take her hand. 'Mr D'Aquanni, thank you. You have no need to apologise. I know what...' She stopped for a second. 'It doesn't matter what I know. We're all fine, Paolo and I are together and our baby is healthy; that's all that matters.'

Nobody moved for a long moment and then Alicia felt compelled against her will to look up. Her eyes clashed with Dante's dark, intense gaze and she couldn't look away. She started shaking her head even before the words came out. 'Dante I'm not—'

'Alicia, please, come with me now.' His voice sounded strained.

Alicia looked from one set of speculative eyes to the other. They didn't need to hear this—this was between her and Dante. She remembered his look just now after seeing the baby and it had hardened and firmed her resolve.

Before walking out of the clinic, though, she went and looked in on her niece for a long emotional moment. Dante watched her from a distance; he didn't trust himself to go back and look at that tiny baby again.

Outside the clinic Alicia felt a curious calm settle over her. Nothing could disguise the fact that seeing the baby—*seeing his baby niece*—had had little or no impact on Dante. And that meant that Alicia had to face facts. She couldn't go on like this. It would kill her.

She turned to face him as he was about to open the car door for her. His easy action angered her. Did he really think she was going to meekly jump into the car, pretend that the last twenty-four hours hadn't happened?

When Alicia didn't move Dante looked at her sharply. 'What is it?'

Something in her expression made ice settle around his heart—the ice that had lodged there when he'd seen baby Lucia. Paolo and Melanie's happiness had been almost too much to bear. It was so alien to him, that image… He needed to get back to terra firma. Away from here. With Alicia. He would take her back with him; they would sort things out, go on from there.

'I'm not going with you.'

Her voice cut through his thoughts. 'What?' He frowned and

then an impatient look crossed his face. 'Of course you are. I have to be back in Rome tonight. Come on, get in, it's freezing.'

Alicia was oblivious to the cold weather, the leaden skies.

She shook her head. 'No, I'm not going back. This is it, Dante. The end.'

His hand fell from the car door. 'Alicia, come on. We can talk about whatever is wrong in the car.'

Whatever is wrong? Where would they start? This had nothing to do with Paolo and Melanie any more. This was *them*. The fact that Dante had been wrong all along was laughably beside the point.

She shook her head and backed away slightly, arms around her belly, her eyes huge.

A feeling moved through him, panic mixed with relief. 'If you want to stay for a few days, that's fine. I can send the plane back to get you when you're ready…' his mouth quirked tiredly '…or you can come economy if you insist, I know how you feel—'

'No!' She had to stop him, had to make him see. 'You don't understand. I mean I'm not coming back—*at all*. I want you to go now. I want to stay here. I know we'll have to see each other again, at the wedding or…or whatever…' already a knife was piercing her heart at that thought '…but that's it, Dante. This affair is over.'

A fierce elemental wave of possessiveness moved through him and he stepped forward. 'No, it's not. You don't say when— *I* do.'

'That's just the problem,' Alicia said sadly. 'You will, one of these days, and I won't be able to bear it.'

He stopped advancing, exactly as she'd known and feared he would. She knew there was only one way to make Dante walk away—the only solution—because he was stubborn and determined and if he thought he could persuade her…she might still be too weak to resist.

She tipped up her chin in that defiant way that had become

so endearing to him but Dante wasn't aware of the subliminal message. He was battling a cave man instinct to grab Alicia and pull her into the car. And yet something was keeping him from moving—she had said she wouldn't be able to *bear it.*

Against his will, he had to ask, 'What do you mean?'

Alicia took a deep breath. 'What I mean, Dante…is that I've been stupid enough to fall in love with you.' Her heart stopped for a brief, hopelessly hopeful, second. But when she saw the way his face leached of colour, the vaguely horror struck expression, she hardened her heart. This pain eclipsed anything she jad experienced before, but somehow she stayed standing.

'You can't have,' he breathed, his mind seizing in shock. 'I never asked you to fall in love with me.'

Alicia would have smiled wryly if she'd had the wherewithal. 'You can't make someone fall in love with you, you can't ask someone to fall in love with you…it's uncontrollable.' She didn't know how she stood in the car park on that cold day and said the following words with such calm.

'The heart wants what the heart wants…and my heart wants you, Dante. But I want it all, not just a temporary arrangement. I want the works. I want to be married, to have children…to know the joy that Melanie and Paolo know…I want to grow old with you. I want the full package…and I know you don't want that; it's glaringly obvious.'

Something cynical lit Dante's eyes at that moment, as if he'd seized on something in her words, and Alicia reacted with unchecked fury. Her arms dropped, she pointed a trembling finger at him. 'Oh, no, you don't, Dante D'Aquanni. Don't you dare reduce what I've said to a cynical justification. I couldn't care less if you were the king of Italy or that street kid grown up and waiting tables in Naples and you know it. So don't you dare try that.' She was shaking with emotion.

His mouth opened and shut. She had caught him—pricelessly. With deadly accuracy. He felt removed from the situation. She was standing there, saying these words and he couldn't *feel* anything. Like when he'd watched Lucia only moments before. As if a granite block was weighing him down inside. Yet again someone was asking him to believe, not to be cynical... and the pain of the last time when he *had* believed was still too memorable. Like a default mode, he went inwards. Self-protection.

He stepped backwards to the car and said with a clipped finality that tore what was left of Alicia's heart to shreds, 'You seem to have it all figured out.'

Alicia nodded. An aching sob built inside her. Dante was remote and calm and controlled. He didn't have a heart. He'd lost it so long ago that now it was irredeemable.

'Can I give you a lift somewhere?'

Just like that, he was already moving on. Alicia couldn't stop a half hysterical gurgle of laughter breaking from her lips, and then a wave of weariness came over her. She shook her head. 'No. Just go, Dante. Go home.'

With barely a backward glance he got into the back of the car. Within seconds the door had shut and it was pulling away out of the car park, leaving her standing there, alone...and contemplating the advantages of very possibly fainting in such close proximity to a clinic.

The mornings were the worst, when she would wake up and reach for Dante, only to find an empty, cold space. And then she would remember. One morning she'd groaned with the pain it had been so acute, and curled up into a ball. And she couldn't help but go over every last bit of that fight they'd had in Milan; she could see now how fantastically coincidental her own admission that they had shared a similar past must have seemed, coming so close on the heels of his story.

She knew instinctively that he'd believed her though when she'd mentioned records and the orphanage because that would have appealed to the logical side of him that would want proof. And, with his apology to Paolo and Melanie, she knew he'd finally accepted the full truth. How could he have looked at that tiny baby—so like Paolo—and not?

But, despite all that, it was useless to obsess over words. He would never let someone into his heart because it was too late. He was full of demons and contradictions.

That week, Alicia had stayed in a hostel near the clinic and in the mornings would rise and wash and go to visit Mel and Paolo. Even though it was obvious that they wondered what had happened, they never asked about her pale face or where Dante was. And then she would go back to the hostel in the afternoons and cry. Non stop. For being so stupid as to fall for a man as damaged as Dante.

At the weekend she returned to the apartment in Oxford to pack up and move out. On Sunday morning she lay in bed and contemplated the cracks and peeling paint of the ceiling. Melanie had asked her to move into the London house with them. But that was Dante's house; there was no way she could do that. She'd look for somewhere nearby and she would have to start looking for work. The door buzzer sounded and Alicia dragged herself out of bed. She felt about a hundred years old and she knew it would be old Mrs Smith from next door, wondering if she could get her some milk from the corner shop because she always called at the same time every day when they were home. She pulled on faded jeans and a sweatshirt.

Alicia pulled the door back, pasting a fake smile on her face. 'Good morning, Mrs Smith.'

The old woman smiled at Alicia. 'I'm so sorry to bother you, pet; it's my hip, in this weather…'

Alicia let her carry on as she pulled on shoes and a coat. 'It's no problem.' *Believe me, you're doing me a favour; I could stay in bed for the rest of my life and never leave…*

As she came back into the little lane that led up to their doors, Alicia was looking at the paper she'd bought, unaware of the men standing at her doorway. She only noticed them when she looked up for a split second to see where she was going. She only saw one man, even though somewhere she had registered others too.

The milk fell from suddenly nerveless hands, breaking open and splashing all over the ground and her shoes. The paper followed. Shock and pain slammed into her and she finally moved for sanctuary, to her door, pushing past, willing herself not to be aware of his presence. 'No...*no,* leave me alone, Dante. Just leave me be.'

She couldn't get the key in the lock because her hand was shaking too much. He plucked it from her hand and turned her to face him. He looked awful. He looked grey; deep lines marked his face, his eyes were bloodshot. She hadn't really taken his appearance in at first, too stunned. All antipathy flew out of the window. She reacted on pure instinct, almost reaching out a hand.

'Dante...my God, what is it, you look—'

'About as bad as you, I'd say.' His voice was hoarse.

She knew she did look bad, after a week of incessant crying over this man who didn't even deserve it. Pain flooded back. She rediscovered her backbone. 'If you've come here just to insult me—'

'I haven't. *Dio*—' he ran a hand through his hair, which seemed to have grown longer in just a week '—isn't it obvious?'

She was tight-lipped, barely holding on to some control. 'Not to me it's not.'

He stood back a little and, perversely, Alicia wanted to grab him and hit him and kiss him all at the same time. He looked to the two men who were beside him and Alicia blanched slightly. And then she recognized them. It was the reporter and photographer from that first night at Dante's villa on Lake Como—the local paparazzi. They were looking dazed, out of place, as if they'd just been beamed from another planet.

Déjà vu made her dizzy. She looked from them to him with what she knew must be a stupid look on her face. 'Why are they here?'

Dante looked grim. 'I brought them with me to bear witness.' His mouth twisted. 'Flew them here on my plane, which is an extravagance you'll just have to forgive me.'

Alicia's mouth opened and closed. And she watched, struck dumb, as Dante knelt down on two knees before her, in a puddle of milk.

'Alicia, I was a fool. A stupid, blind idiot. I walked away from you and told myself I didn't need you, didn't want you, *didn't love you...*'

Alicia was feeling light-headed. Still they didn't touch. He was looking up at her and she couldn't move.

'You were right. The heart knows what it wants, and my heart wants you. Needs you. Loves you. The past week has shown me what a future without you in it would be like...' He shook his head and, amazingly, moisture glistened in his eyes. 'I could hardly last a week, how did I ever think I could last a lifetime? It took the thought of seeing you at some family function, but not being able to touch you or talk to you to finally crack open my heart, and when I thought about how I would feel if I saw you with another man...' He shuddered visibly. 'Not even seeing my own baby niece, who is called after my mother, could do it.'

He bowed his head for a moment before looking up again. 'When this all blew up, it had such parallels to what had happened before...I *was* jealous that Paolo had the gall to fall in love and believe that everything could be OK. With no cynicism, no suspicion. And then you came along, like a tiny tornado, and from that first moment...I was yours. But I fought it—fought it all the way, right to the bitter end. I twisted everything you did to see the worst possible aspect because I was too much of a coward to trust in something good. To be optimistic.'

Alicia felt her own eyes start to water and she furiously blinked to keep it out. Her throat swallowed convulsively. This had to be a dream but the presence of the other two men grounded her in reality. Fantastic reality. Unreal reality.

Dante took her chilled hands in his. 'Please tell me it's not too late.'

Alicia shook her head, her eyes watering in earnest now. She didn't know what to say, where to start. Her heart felt fit to burst and she was overwhelmed that he was here, saying the words she'd longed to hear. Maybe she took too long to speak because Dante's face got bleaker and bleaker.

He rose like a dark demon, his face stark with pain. 'I won't let you send me away. If you meant what you said last week, then you can't have—'

Alicia reached up and put a hand over his mouth. She smiled tremulously through her tears. 'I'm trying to tell you that it's *not* too late.'

The relief and sheer joy that crossed Dante's face made her feel even weaker. He pulled her up, holding her high, and she put hands on either side of his face, pressing small kisses everywhere. It was frantic and impassioned. She could vaguely sense movement near them and it was only when she pulled back that she noticed the photographer snapping feverishly, the reporter taking notes.

She wrapped her arms tight around his neck and pressed her face into it, breathing his scent deep. It was like coming home, like a balm to her ravaged soul. She whispered in his ear, 'Do you think they could leave now?'

She felt him nod, his voice was low and husky. 'I wanted to make you believe, to show you that you could trust me.'

Alicia smiled a watery smile and pressed another kiss to his lips. Then he turned and spoke to the men. 'OK, that's it, you've got your story. I don't need witnesses for the next bit.'

Alicia couldn't believe he was putting his heart on his sleeve so publicly. *For her.* He pulled back to see her face, momentary tension in his body, and Alicia revelled in it. Shyly she smiled, her eyes on his, telling him everything he needed to know.

He was about to slide the key in the door when Alicia noticed something.

'Mrs Smith's milk!'

Dante rolled his eyes and lowered her down his body slowly. 'If we go and get milk for Mrs Smith, then can I ask you to marry me?'

She nodded happily.

The bemused paparazzi sent a shot of Dante D'Aquanni and Alicia Parker walking hand in hand to the local corner shop to get milk around the world. And, less than twenty-four hours later, the story broke of a winter wedding to take place at Dante's Lake Como villa.

Three and a half years later...

Dante picked up the cuddly toy from the floor of the hall. He stopped with one foot on the bottom step and looked around. A buggy stood just inside the villa's main door. The detritus and evidence of a young person lay everywhere.

A young person and now an even tinier one.

His heart swelled as he looked up the stairs and started to climb. To think that he had ever thought he couldn't experience this, would have denied himself this. The *love and fulfilment of a soul mate, a family...*

He shivered inwardly at how close he had come to shutting it all out.

Just then his wife appeared at the top of the stairs. She was doing up the buttons of her dress. She smiled and he felt an answering one rise up from his feet as he unconsciously speeded up. She looked a little tired, a little plumper around the middle, her breasts were bigger from nursing, and he felt that ever present desire surge through him as strong as the first time he'd ever kissed her. He could truly say he'd never seen anything or anyone more beautiful.

When he reached her he bent and effortlessly plucked her off her bare feet and into his arms. She looked up and rolled her eyes in mock irritation as he strode down the hall to their bedroom.

'Dante D'Aquanni, when will you stop carting me around like a bag of potatoes? I have two feet, two legs...'

The door shut behind them and all that could be heard for some time was the sound of low voices, muted laughter, growing passion and then blissful peace. At least for a while...

Back in his bed—and he's better than ever!

Whether you shared his bed for one night or five
years, certain men are impossible to forget!
He might be your ex, but when you're back in his
bed, the passion is not just hot, it's scorching!

CLAIMED BY THE
ROGUE BILLIONAIRE
by **Trish Wylie**

Available January 2009
Book #2794

*Look for more Exclusively His novels
from Harlequin Presents in 2009!*

HARLEQUIN *Presents*

Demure but defiant...
Can three international playboys
tame their disobedient brides?

Lynne Graham

presents

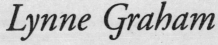

Proud, masculine and passionate, these men are used
to having it all. In stories filled with drama, desire
and secrets of the past, find out how these arrogant
husbands capture their hearts.

THE GREEK TYCOON'S DISOBEDIENT BRIDE
Available December 2008, Book #2779

THE RUTHLESS MAGNATE'S VIRGIN MISTRESS
Available January 2009, Book #2787

THE SPANISH BILLIONAIRE'S PREGNANT WIFE
Available February 2009, Book #2795

REQUEST YOUR FREE BOOKS!

HARLEQUIN *Presents*®

2 FREE NOVELS PLUS 2 FREE GIFTS!

PASSION GUARANTEED SEDUCTION

YES! Please send me 2 FREE Harlequin Presents® novels and my 2 FREE gifts (gifts are worth about $10). After receiving them, if I don't wish to receive any more books, I can return the shipping statement marked "cancel". If I don't cancel, I will receive 6 brand-new novels every month and be billed just $4.05 per book in the U.S. or $4.74 per book in Canada, plus 25¢ shipping and handling per book and applicable taxes, if any*. That's a savings of close to 15% off the cover price! I understand that accepting the 2 free books and gifts places me under no obligation to buy anything. I can always return a shipment and cancel at any time. Even if I never buy another book, the two free books and gifts are mine to keep forever.   106 HDN ERRW 306 HDN ERRL

Name	(PLEASE PRINT)	
Address		Apt. #
City	State/Prov.	Zip/Postal Code

Signature (if under 18, a parent or guardian must sign)

Mail to the **Harlequin Reader Service:**
IN U.S.A.: P.O. Box 1867, Buffalo, NY 14240-1867
IN CANADA: P.O. Box 609, Fort Erie, Ontario L2A 5X3

Not valid to current subscribers of Harlequin Presents books.

Want to try two free books from another line?
Call 1-800-873-8635 or visit www.morefreebooks.com.

* Terms and prices subject to change without notice. N.Y. residents add applicable sales tax. Canadian residents will be charged applicable provincial taxes and GST. Offer not valid in Quebec. This offer is limited to one order per household. All orders subject to approval. Credit or debit balances in a customer's account(s) may be offset by any other outstanding balance owed by or to the customer. Please allow 4 to 6 weeks for delivery. Offer available while quantities last.

Your Privacy: Harlequin Books is committed to protecting your privacy. Our Privacy Policy is available online at www.eHarlequin.com or upon request from the Reader Service. From time to time we make our lists of customers available to reputable third parties who may have a product or service of interest to you. If you would prefer we not share your name and address, please check here. ☐

HP08R

EXTRA

HIS VIRGIN MISTRESS
Bedded by command!

He's wealthy, commanding, with the self-assurance of a man who knows he has power. He's used to sophisticated, confident women who fit easily into his glamorous world.

She's an innocent virgin, inexperienced and awkward, yet to find a man worthy of her love.

Swept off her feet and into his bed, she'll be shown the most exquisite pleasure— and he'll demand she be his mistress!

Don't miss any of the fabulous stories this month in Presents EXTRA!